CHRISTMAS IN KINGSBURY

A Novella

RUSSELL HABERMANN

Text copyright © 2025 by Russell Habermann

All rights reserved.

No part of this book may be reproduced in any form or by any electronic or mechanical means, including information storage and retrieval systems, without written permission from the author, except for the use of brief quotations in a book review.

Print ISBN: 979-8-264511-35-6

For the residents of Proctor, Minnesota

MONDAY, DECEMBER 19

One

Kara tries to muster Christmas cheer as she takes a seat—and a deep breath.

"We've made it to the final countdown!" Kara says.

The members of the Kingsbury Christmas Festival Planning Committee don't seem to feel the excitement.

Yikes, she thinks, *tough crowd.*

"So today's meeting," she continues, "is about those final details, making sure everything comes together just right. Is there anything anyone wants to add to the agenda before we dive in?"

Kara waits a beat, and the silence echoing through the meeting room in Kingsbury Moose Lodge is deafening.

"Fantastic!" Kara says, then she catches Frank Amundson shaking his head in disapproval. "Frank, do you have something to add?"

"Nope," Frank says without looking at Kara.

Kara wonders why Frank is even involved. He's been planning the Christmas Festival ever since it began and has always been co-chair of the planning committee. And sure, she's heard good things about him—he's very generous in the community, owns Kingsbury Roofing, and serves as president of the Kingsbury Community Club. But while working alongside Kara, Frank has been a downright Scrooge.

"Okay," Kara says, "let's start with a few quick updates." She rattles off about confirming the list of kids' activities, the food trucks, a special appearance by Santa, and "The Holi-DJ". "I'm also going to do some final promotion at the City Council meeting this Wednesday, confirm our tabling vendors, and pick up the special order of string lights from Kingsbury Tool and Supply. I'm installing the extra lights on light poles in Carlson Square tomorrow afternoon. Who's available to lend a hand?"

Absolute crickets.

"It won't even feel like work," Kara says. "We can grab coffees from Tom's Café, play some music… anyone?"

"You know I would," says Dottie Short, Kara's second-grade teacher from twenty years ago. "I'm just not much use with the physical labor anymore." She jostles her cane to demonstrate the point.

"That's okay, Dottie. I appreciate you considering it." Kara looks around the room and says, "Well, I'll plan to be there at three o'clock tomorrow afternoon. We'll have some daylight to install the lights, then can make sure everything works when it gets dark."

Kara keeps the meeting plugging along for thirty minutes, and it takes everything in her to keep going.

She never involves herself with community affairs, and this group is demonstrating why. The lack of passion is absolutely draining! Kara swears she can feel any zeal she had when she originally stepped up to volunteer being leached away with every meeting, every task, every interaction.

But Kara is committed to pulling off the best version of the Kingsbury Christmas Festival possible in memory of her late brother, Tom.

Thinking about her brother and how he organized the Festival for five years, Kara asks herself, *How did Tom deal with the lack of enthusiasm?* She recalls how he took the Festival from a simple bonfire and sing-along in Carlson Square to a true community event. By Tom's last Festival two years ago, people treated it as a kind of Kingsbury homecoming—with attendees from as near as Duluth and as far as the Twin Cities. But despite how loved Tom's Festival was, Kara now knows his ideas faced their fair share of resistance.

"With that," Kara says with a smile, "we're all set for the Christmas Festival! Please be in Carlson Square for setting up on Friday by four o'clock at the latest. This meeting is adjourned. Thank you!"

Some committee members leave right away while others—like Frank—chat idly about God-knows-what, since they sure weren't interested in speaking up during the meeting.

"You do such a nice job," Dottie says to Kara. "Thank you for helping lead the group this year."

Kara sighs. "It's not an easy task," she says.

"Oh, no," Dottie says. "Us northern Minnesota folks are tough nuts to crack sometimes—especially the breed from Kingsbury. But you're doing a wonderful job."

"Thanks," Kara says.

Kara recalls how Dottie told her about being involved with the Christmas Festival since it started thirty-five years ago. *Maybe she has some insight,* she thinks.

"While I have you, do you think this is all going well?" Kara asks. "I mean, compared to other years?"

"Well, last year was a scramble after Tom passed unexpectedly, so this is much better than that," Dottie says. "To be honest, I think it's a feat we have anything at all. But the things you're planning with the activities and Santa and all, they're beyond what we ever dreamed for this event way back when."

"That's good," Kara says. "I just don't understand why no one says anything in the meetings."

"I think it's because you're just so prepared," Dottie says. "You're so thoughtful and come with your agendas and you have answers to everything. I suppose sometimes I think, 'Well, why am I even here? Kara has this all under control!'"

Dottie smiles warmly, but this line of thinking doesn't make Kara feel better. *I don't want to plan the whole event myself*, Kara thinks.

"How are your folks doing, by the way?" Dottie asks. "The holidays can be a hard time after losing someone."

"They're good," Kara says. "They always keep busy with the coffee shop."

"Your mom is like a little Energizer Bunny!" Dottie laughs. "And your brother and sister?"

"Yes," Kara says, "they're doing well. Jordan is living in Tom's old house in town here, and Suzy is finishing up nursing school this spring. She's supposed to be back in town today for holiday break."

"I just love the Bell family!" Dottie says. "I had all four of you kids for second grade, and those were my absolute favorite years of teaching." Dottie pulls on her jacket, pushes off the table to get herself standing, and uses her cane to travel toward the door. "You make sure you greet everyone for me," she winks.

"I will," Kara smiles.

"And you make sure you keep your chin up," Dottie says. "I admire you keeping up Tom's legacy by stepping out of your comfort zone and taking this on. The Festival's going to be different from when he ran things, but that doesn't mean it's any worse. In fact, some people may think it's even better."

"I don't know about all that," Kara says.

"I do!" Dottie says. "Just remember, the only opinions that matter are the opinions of people who believe in you."

Two

Jordan arrives at Carlson Square just before five o'clock. It's dark already, and he tries to get a lay of the land before the press conference kicks off.

The lights glowing from inside of each business around the Square turn off in succession as their workers close shop for the night. And the mismatched streetlamps—some a sharp white and others a soft amber—illuminate the Square and its assemblage of a dozen or so people awaiting the event.

Jordan's assignment from *The Kingsbury Gazette* is to cover the launch of a weeklong treasure hunt coinciding with the Kingsbury Christmas Festival. The whole thing is a mystery—apparently only shared by word of mouth. His publisher-editor didn't have much more to share besides when Jordan would need to report to Carlson Square. He just needs to find out what's going on, quickly write an article, and turn it around as soon as possible for this Thursday's issue.

"Hey," Jordan hears from behind him.

He turns his head and sees Beatrice Halvorson, his older brother Tom's best friend since kindergarten.

And Jordan's lifelong crush.

"What are you doing here?" he asks with a smile.

"I needed to come see what all the fuss was about," Beatrice says. "Plus, there's nothing else to do in this town."

She's not wrong, Jordan thinks. He lived in Kingsbury for eighteen years before moving to Madison for college and then to Chicago for a few years of work. He knows firsthand that this town isn't exactly a metropolis. But he didn't realize how dull it truly is until moving back last year and taking a job at the *Gazette*. Now he can confirm there isn't much in Kingsbury for people to leave their homes for, especially in the doldrums of winter.

"What have you heard about this thing anyway?" Beatrice asks.

"Just that there's a treasure hunt for the Christmas Festival," Jordan says. "You?"

"That there are five clues, one posted at five o'clock each night this week," she says. "Hey, have you heard if Jessica is coming home for the holidays?"

Jessica Lindquist. She dates—or dated—Jordan's brother for several years and became close friends with Beatrice too. But after Tom's death, Jessica took a job in the Twin Cities and hasn't been back to Kingsbury.

"No," Jordan says. "And wouldn't you know more than I would anyway?"

Beatrice sighs. "That's the thing," she says. "I've been trying to reach out and haven't heard from her. I was hoping she'd at least come visit her parents for the holidays so we could catch up."

"Would she even let you know she's in town if she did?" Jordan asks. "She's been kind of discrete since Tom…"

"Valid point," Beatrice says.

They hear a rolling cymbal fill the air, and for the first time Jordan notices speakers set up around the Square.

"Does that mean it's starting?" Jordan asks.

Beatrice shrugs. "It must," she says.

A group of twenty boys in white choir robes float into the Square, organizing themselves into choral formation in front of the small crowd.

Music from the speakers cues them, and a boy in the front row starts to sing the first refrain of "Carol of the Bells". The song builds and envelops Carlson Square, causing some of the people closing businesses across the street to stop and listen to the haunting sound of children's voices in the night air.

When the song wraps up, the small group assembled in the Square—maybe mostly the boys' parents?—provide a smattering of applause.

Jordan turns to Beatrice, and he finds her walking up to where the boys are standing.

What is she doing? Jordan thinks.

Beatrice holds up a microphone and says, "Welcome to the official launch of the Kingsbury Christmas Festival treasure hunt!"

I thought she didn't know about this, Jordan thinks.

Beatrice continues, "This is a one-time event that will span the next week. Each day from now until Friday, a clue to where the treasure is hidden on public property within the city of Kingsbury will be revealed here in Carlson Square. Please be aware that the treasure is hidden, but it is *not* buried; if you're thinking of trying to dig up the frozen ground on public property, please don't."

A few chuckles bubble up from the crowd.

"What is the treasure?" Beatrice asks. "The item you should seek is a small token—we are not disclosing *what* the token is, but it's an item of value, and you'll know it when you find it. The person who finds this mystery token and returns it to me will be named the sole benefactor of the estate of Thomas Valentine Bell."

What?! Jordan thinks. *Tom's estate? This can't be right.*

And yet he knows full well that Beatrice is the executor of his older brother's estate. She is one of few who knows what is *right* when it comes to his brother's will.

"For those familiar with the Christmas Festival, Tom Bell helped organize the event for five years before his passing. Before Tom passed, he disclosed within his will that distribution of his assets be determined by a public treasure hunt to coincide with the Kingsbury Christmas Festival. The value of Mr. Bell's estate is estimated at over two hundred fifty thousand dollars."

Hushed whispers rise from the crowd.

"This is quite a sum," Beatrice says. "Please be assured that this is not a joke." She pauses to pull out a stack of half-sheet papers. "Official rules for the treasure hunt are available on these handouts, which are available immediately and will be available throughout the week at the city clerk's office in Kingsbury City Hall. Now, without further to do, the first clue."

Beatrice steps aside, and the boys' choir starts to sing a flourish of melody and harmonies as a large, thirty-foot-tall banner unravels with the first clue of the treasure hunt:

There's nothing more magic
Than a season's first snow—
When life seems suspended
And time seems to slow,
When dreams feel closer

And burdens feel lost.
It's really too bad
Magic comes at a cost.

There's a moment of silence while everyone, including the members of the boys' choir, reads the clue and then confers with their neighbors about its meaning.

Jordan thinks, *How is that a clue?*

And then the full situation hits him. Number one, Tom's estate is worth more than a quarter-million dollars! *Does that include the house where I've been living for the past year?* Jordan wonders.

And number two, Tom is leaving his estate to whoever wins a random community treasure hunt?! Jordan knows his brother was eccentric, but this is a whole new level.

And then Jordan realizes he still has a job to do for the *Gazette*.

He walks quickly up to Beatrice before anyone else can approach her.

"Can I get an interview?" Jordan asks.

Beatrice takes a beat to smile at him. "Of course," she says.

"Thanks," Jordan says. "And this is for an article in the *Gazette*."

"I figured," Beatrice nods.

"So," Jordan starts, "tell me how the whole treasure hunt idea came along."

"As you know, I'm the executor of Tom's will. In the event of his demise," Beatrice says, "Tom stipulated that distribution of his assets be determined by a public treasure hunt to coincide with the Kingsbury Christmas Festival."

"Yes," Jordan says, "that's exactly what you told the whole group."

"Legally, I'm required to be precise with the language," Beatrice says.

"Okay," Jordan says. "What kind of impact will this have on Friday's Christmas Festival?"

"We won't know until the Festival happens," Beatrice says. "But I can imagine there may be greater incentive to attend and see the final clue revealed—if the treasure isn't found by Friday."

"Knowing that this article's issue of the *Gazette* will hit newsstands this Thursday, what do you want our readers to know about the hunt?" Jordan asks.

"Tom loved Kingsbury," Beatrice says. "He would just want everybody to have fun and safely enjoy this opportunity."

"And one more question," Jordan says. "Tom died over a year ago. As executor of the will, why haven't you told anybody—*especially* his family—about how this was all going down?"

Beatrice frowns. "Off the record," she says, "I wanted to, but Tom wanted everything to be a surprise."

"So why," Jordan asks, "did you act like you didn't know anything about the hunt when we were talking a few minutes ago?"

Beatrice takes a deep breath. "The will was specific," she says, "that I couldn't say anything until the hunt was officially launched. I'm sorry, Jordan."

Jordan shakes his head. "Tom sure knows how to haunt a person's life," he says.

Beatrice says, "You have no idea."

Three

Suzy takes a deep breath and pushes through the door of Tom's Café. Everything about the place—the tinkle of the bell above the door, the smell of pistachio muffins, the whir of the espresso machine—is like a warm hug. But she's been dreading this day for the past three weeks.

"Suze!" her mom says from behind the counter, ditching a customer to run and give her daughter a squeeze. "How was the trip?"

"Fast," Suzy says with a smile.

"Good," her mom says, patting her back. "The trip home should always feel shorter than the trip away. What can I get you?" she asks, leading her daughter toward the counter.

Suzy inhales deeply. "Nothing right now," she says. "Help the customers. I'll go say hi to dad."

Suzy wanders into the back of the shop to her dad's office.

"Hey there," she says from the doorway.

"Ah," her dad says as he stands and folds his arms around Suzy. "The birthday girl is home."

"My birthday isn't until Friday," Suzy says.

"Which makes this your birthday *week*," Suzy's dad says. "What do I always say?"

"Holidays," Suzy recites, "aren't about the actual day."

"They're about the countdown," dad and daughter say simultaneously.

"And your *golden* birthday week, no less," he says, sitting back down at his desk. "I can't believe my baby is almost twenty-three."

Suzy rolls her eyes. "Okay," she says.

"Especially when *I'm* only thirty-six," her dad jokes.

Suzy just shakes her head.

"So," he says, slapping his hands together, "how did finals go?"

"Good!" Suzy says, and she instantly hopes she doesn't sound too enthusiastic.

Her dad leans back in his office chair. "Only one semester left. How are we feeling?" he asks.

"Good," she lies again. "It's nothing I can't handle."

"That's my girl," her dad says.

"Dan," Suzy's mom sticks her head in the office, "don't catch up with Suzy without me. She's going to tell you everything and then forget that I haven't heard."

"She's hardly giving me any information," Suzy's dad says.

"Suze," her mom says, "would you hate giving me a hand up front?"

Suzy genuinely smiles. "I would love it," she says.

The only place Suzy ever feels at ease is behind the counter at Tom's Café. When she sees a regular customer, it's more like visiting a friend. When someone is being difficult, it's excitement. In Suzy's world, Tom's Café is a big pair of rose-tinted glasses. It's where she belongs. And if she had her way, she would ditch any idea of the nursing profession and take over the shop herself one day.

Suzy pulls on an apron, and everything seems right in the world.

"You work the counter, I work the bar?" Suzy's mom asks.

"Sounds like a plan," Suzy smiles.

When she reaches the counter, Suzy looks around to see if anything changed since she last posted up here before Labor Day. And everything looks as expected—that is, except for a golden envelope slipped right underneath the register.

Suzy pulls the envelope out and sees her name scrawled across the front in lilting handwriting. She holds it up to her mom. "What's this?" she asks.

Her mom walks over and takes a look. "I'm not sure," she says with a shrug. "But it looks like it's for you."

Suzy rips the envelope and pulls out a card.

"'This week you will receive twenty-three gifts,'" Suzy reads out loud. "'Expect the first when the bell tolls one.'"

"That's sweet. Is this Michael's doing?" Suzy's mom asks, referencing Suzy's longtime boyfriend.

"I'm not sure," Suzy says. "'When the bell tolls one'… Why does that sound familiar?"

Expect the first when the bell tolls one.

"Oh!" Suzy remembers. "It's from *A Christmas Carol*. The ghosts visit Scrooge at one in the morning, right?"

"If you say so," her mom shrugs. "It must be a golden birthday surprise. Twenty-three presents?"

"Or a Christmas prank," Suzy says.

***

Despite her best avoidance efforts, Suzy can't seem to shake the warning about one o'clock, so she gets antsy as the clock spins into afternoon.

A few minutes before one, the bell above the door tinkles as Suzy's boyfriend Mike walks into the shop.

Suzy navigates herself directly into Mike's arms. "I missed you," Suzy says and kisses him.

With Suzy going to nursing school in the Twin Cities, the one big fear between Suzy and Mike was how distance might drive a wedge between them. And sure, they decided to go on a break during her freshman year. But other than that, they were unquestionably loyal to each other—even from one hundred fifty miles away.

"I missed you, too," Mike says, giving her a squeeze before pulling away.

"Did you come with my first gift?" Suzy rolls her eyes.

Mike smiles at Suzy, then becomes confused. "What do you mean?" he asks.

Suzy grabs the card from behind the counter and shows Mike. She asks, "This isn't from you?"

"No," Mike says. He reads the note. "Why is it so ominous? And twenty-three gifts? That's a lot."

"Huh," Suzy frowns. "Who could it be from then?"

Mike shrugs. "Someone with a lot of money apparently," he says. "Unless they're all little dollar store gifts or something?"

Then the bell above the shop door tinkles again.

A group of four people—two men and two women—decked out in traditional Victorian clothing bustle into the door of Tom's Café.

A man from the group steps forward. "Miss Suzy Bell, I presume," he says to Suzy.

"Yeah?" Suzy asks.

The man hands Suzy a small golden card with the same lilting handwriting from the envelope by the register.

"'Here we come'," she reads out loud to Mike.

"Okay," Mike says, "what is going—"

And the Victorian carolers start singing "Here We Come A-wassailing", to the amusement of some café patrons—and the annoyance of others.

After eight verses, the men bow, the ladies curtsy, and they all leave the shop as quickly as they came. The patrons give them a round of applause, and Suzy feels her cheeks flush with embarrassment.

"Okay," Mike says, "what is a wassail?"

"I don't know," Suzy says. "Do you think that was one of the presents?"

"I mean," Mike says, "they *did* arrive when the bell tolled one."

"Christmas is the absolute worst," Suzy says.

And she means it. With her birthday on December twenty-third, Suzy feels like she pulled the short straw of birthdays.

As the youngest sibling of four growing up, she never had a day that was all hers. And even when her birthday rolled around, any party she had also doubled as some kind of holiday gathering. Was she bitter about it? Yes. Did she have a right to be? Absolutely.

"So what are your plans tonight?" Mike asks. "We should go out. I want to hear how the semester wrapped up."

"Oh," Suzy says, withering at the thought of school. "I actually want to try a few new dessert recipes at the shop this week. So I have to run to the store after work."

"I can come with you," Mike says.

"No," Suzy says, "I just want to make a quick run after I'm done here."

"I can come over after," Mike offers.

"No, that's all right," Suzy says. "I'd just like to have a quiet night. Maybe another time."

Suzy can see Mike's confusion, and she wants to make it right. But the truth? She just doesn't want to hang out with Mike—not when she has to keep a secret from him.

"Tomorrow night?" Mike asks.

Suzy shrugs. "We can talk about it," she says.

Mike furrows his brow at her. "Is something wrong?" he asks.

Yes, Suzy thinks. *I dropped out of nursing school, which is everything my mom and dad ever wanted for me, and I don't want to wreck our first full holiday season without Tom by breaking my parents' hearts.*

"No," Suzy says. "I think I'm just tired from the trip."

Four

Kara walks into The Wheelhouse, and she's enveloped in a blanket of warm air. *Even a short walk across the street is enough to freeze someone solid in Kingsbury*, she thinks.

Walking to the reception counter, Kara unbuttons her coat and looks around the newly renovated restaurant. She knows it well from her childhood, when the building hosted a fast-food chain and then a couple locally owned eateries—a bakery, a pizza place, an ice cream shop. She expects to see the remnants of these former lives barely masked with new décor, but it seems whoever renovated the place did away with the old completely. Gone are the plastic booths and drop ceiling tiles, and here are the dark wood furniture pieces and exposed black-sprayed ceilings. To Kara, it combines Kingsbury's industrial railroad history and its modern tastes in a way people rarely pull off well.

"Hey, have you been helped?" a voice says from behind the reception counter.

Kara is flustered by the man standing in front of her. Tall, fit, warm eyes, great hair.

He must not be from here, she thinks.

"Um," she says, looking over at the people occupying the seating area. "I... sorry." She shakes her head. "No, I haven't. But I'm meeting someone, and I'm not sure if she's here yet."

He bites his lip and squints one eye. "Are you Kara?" he asks.

"Yes?" Kara asks instead of says.

"Wendy sent you," he says and extends his hand to shake hers. "I'm Brent. She told me to expect you. Let me just let the staff know."

He disappears into the kitchen, and Kara is left with a thousand questions. But mainly, *What did you do now, Wendy?*

Kara looks at the door and considers making her escape, but Brent reappears too quickly.

"Our booth is right over here," he says, leading the way as she stiffly follows him.

Kara drops into the booth opposite Brent and can't help asking anymore. "So... where's Wendy?" she says.

His face goes blank, looking suddenly unsure. "Wendy said she wanted me to meet you," he says. "Did she not..."

"She did not," Kara confirms. "She asked me to meet *her* here for coffee."

"Ah," Brent says, folding his hands in front of him. "Does she do this kind of thing often?"

"You mean set her friends up on a surprise meeting with a handsome stranger?" Kara asks. "No."

Brent smiles. "Handsome?"

"Ha! I mean, objectively handsome," Kara says, "in that classically handsome sort of way."

Yikes, Kara thinks.

"But... handsomeness *is* in the eye of the beholder," she says, flustered and taking a deep breath. "This can't be the first time you've heard it."

"Well, we just met, so maybe this is getting too deep," Brent says. "But a girl I was once talking to told my mom

I was handsome. My mom relayed this to me, then said I wouldn't find many people who would agree."

"Your mom called you ugly?" Kara asks.

"Well, she didn't call me handsome," Brent says, shaking his head. "By the way, if this wasn't what you were expecting, we don't need to do this."

Kara looks at him across the table. *He is pretty cute,* she thinks. *I'm going to kill Wendy.*

"Now that I'm here," Kara concedes, "I guess I wouldn't mind having a coffee."

She settles in as a server comes over and takes their order. And after Kara sips some extremely decent coffee from the kind of solid clay mugs she likes, she feels her heart settle down in her chest.

"So, you work here?" Kara asks.

Brent grins. "I own the place," he says.

Kara looks around the restaurant and its cozy ruggedness. "You did all this?" she asks.

"I mean, I didn't do *all* of it," he says, "but this is the vision I had in mind."

"When I walked in, I was expecting to see the same plastic booths and a neon rainbow ice cream light on the wall," Kara says. "I'm impressed."

"Well, the neon rainbow ice cream light didn't really fit the new aesthetic," Brent says.

"I should think not," Kara says. "You're not from Kingsbury, right?"

"Correct," Brent says.

"So how did you land here?" she asks.

"It's kind of a long story," Brent says. "But the short version is that I went to college in Duluth, then I went back home to the Cities and... I just missed it up here. So I picked up and moved on a whim. Had a food truck for a few years in Duluth and then decided I wanted to put down some roots."

"In Kingsbury?" Kara says.

"The building was available for the right price, and Kingsbury didn't have its own casual dining spot. It has plenty of bars, takeout pizza, a coffee shop, and now... The Wheelhouse." He shrugs. "How about you?"

Kara grimaces. "I'm from here," she says, "and my parents own the aforementioned coffee shop down the street."

"No kidding," Brent says. "Tom's Café?"

"One and the same," Kara says.

"That's a great place," he says. "And that's your mom behind the counter?"

"Yes," Kara shakes her head, "she likes to call herself the 'Chief Operating Officer'. My dad does the business side of it and just calls himself 'the help'."

"Your dad must be Tom then," Brent says, leaning back into the booth.

Kara scrunches up her nose. "No, Tom is my older brother. He was a baby when my parents opened the place almost thirty years ago."

"Well, he's gotta take it over when they retire," Brent says. "I mean, his name's all over it."

Kara looks into her coffee. She hates this part.

"He actually passed away last year right before Christmas," she says.

"Oh," Brent winces. "I'm sorry."

"He was a paramedic," Kara says, "and a car didn't stop at the scene of a car crash."

"That's awful," Brent says.

"Yeah. But Tom wouldn't have wanted us to dwell on it," she says. "So we move forward."

Just then, Kara sees Frank Amundson walking into The Wheelhouse. A server seats him and his friend a few tables away from Kara and Brent.

"So do you work at your parents' shop too?" Brent asks.

Even though Kara is distracted by Frank's presence, she tries to focus on Brent and ignore whatever conversation Frank is having.

"I work in accounting with the school district," Kara says. "I've been there about three years. But before that, I helped at my parents' shop. I went to school for accounting, and my dad helped show me how to apply the concepts in the real world. I might have given him a few pointers too," she smiles.

Frank's voice echoes over to Kara's table. "And she has no idea what she's doing," Frank says. "She comes in here and tries to take over everything."

Is he talking about me? Kara thinks.

"I'm sure she intends well," Frank's friend says.

"I don't care what she intends," Frank replies. "She has zero respect for thirty-five years of tradition."

"Is something wrong?" Brent asks Kara.

Kara tries to focus on what's happening at her own booth. "No, it's fine," she says. "Just a small town," she shrugs.

"Then why don't you just quit?" Frank's friend asks.

"I should," Frank says. "It's worse than when her brother took everything over."

Worse than when her brother took over? Kara thinks.

Kara can stand people talking about her, but people dragging her late brother's name through the mud crosses a line.

"Excuse me," Kara says to Frank.

Frank and his friend turn to look in her direction. Since Frank doesn't seem surprised to see her, maybe he knew she was within earshot all along.

"Do you know them?" Brent asks.

Kara looks at Brent and exhales, then turns back to Frank. "What do you mean, 'It's worse than when her brother took everything over'?"

Frank puts down the menu he was holding and says, "I mean that the Christmas Festival would be better off if your brother—and you—would leave it alone. You act like you're trying to save the whole town. I mean, food trucks and a DJ? Who are you kidding? This is Kingsbury."

"Is it so wrong to want better for this town?" Kara asks.

"Better?" Frank says. "By whose definition?"

"No one is making you be part of the Christmas Festival Committee," Kara says.

"I *started* the Christmas Festival Committee," Frank tells her. "And you'd be wise to remember that."

"And if you want the Festival to continue for years to come," Kara says, "you'd be wise to loosen the reins and pass it onto the next generation."

"Maybe I don't want to pass it onto a generation that has lost all concept of what the Festival is about," Frank says.

"It's not *difficult*," Kara says, "to understand what the *Christmas* Festival is about."

"Then how are you getting it so wrong?" Frank asks.

Brent leans across the table to Kara. "Maybe you two can continue this in the side room," Brent says to her.

And suddenly, she recognizes that all eyes in the dining room are either looking at her and Frank—or actively trying to avoid them.

"There's no need for that," Frank says, standing up. "This conversation is over. And so is my involvement with *Kara Bell presents The Christmas Festival*." He pulls his jacket off his chair and heads toward the door. His friend continues to sit at the table, perusing the menu and acting as if nothing just happened.

"Are you okay?" Brent asks Kara.

She takes a deep breath. "Just another Monday," she says. "But I think I better be going." Kara reaches for her wallet to grab some cash.

"It's on me," Brent says.

"Thank you," Kara says as she gets up. "I'm sorry about… all that." And she beelines for the door.

I'm going to kill Wendy, Kara thinks.

Five

Jordan wraps his knuckle on Doug White's doorframe and pokes his head into the office. "Are you ready for me?" Jordan asks.

Doug swivels around in his ancient leather chair—the kind with brass rivets—and waves Jordan in.

The offices of *The Kingsbury Gazette*, housed in a hundred-year-old building once ordered from a Sears catalogue, contains the history and heritage of Kingsbury itself. Or at least it smells that way. With the shop's original printing press and a century of weekly print newspapers being archived in the paint-chipped building, the place—both the publication and the building—are community institutions.

And Jordan is grateful he found a place at the *Gazette* after returning to town. He knows he's better off for spending the past year working for a small-town newspaper.

His bank account, however, may disagree.

Doug motions to a chair opposite his desk, stacked with back copies of the *Gazette*. "Throw those aside and take a seat," he says.

Once Jordan settles in, Doug leans back in his chair and tents his fingers. "I really enjoyed your story," Doug says. "Insightful, informative, a personal spin. And you turned it around within an hour."

"The story wrote itself," Jordan says.

"Stories don't write themselves," Doug says, waving Jordan off. "You're too good for this place."

Jordan shakes his head. "You're too kind," he says.

"No, seriously," Doug says, sitting up and rolling his chair closer to the desk. "If my writing was as strong as yours, I wouldn't be hanging around this place. I mean, no offense to Kingsbury, but it's small potatoes. You're the kind of person Kingsbury raises and then sends out into the world as an ambassador for what a small town can produce."

"Doug—" Jordan says.

"I don't appreciate false modesty, young man," Doug says. "I know you wanted to be here for your family after Tom, but don't you think it's time to fly the nest?"

Jordan mulls over what Doug is trying to get at, then decides to just follow his boss's lead.

"I've thought about it," Jordan says, "but it just hasn't felt right. And truthfully, it didn't feel right the entire time I was away either. 'There's no place like home' and all that."

"You know, they also say 'You can't go home again'," Doug posits.

Jordan pauses and tries to search Doug for what he's really trying to say.

"I wish you would just come out with it," Jordan finally says.

"I always had a knack for burying the lead," Doug huffs. "Here's the headline: we put up a good fight against the internet, but the time has come for *The Kingsbury Gazette* to surrender."

Jordan sinks. In his head, he knew this day would come. But did he truly believe it in his heart?

Adding insult to injury, Doug spells it out plainly: "Next week's issue will be our last, and by January first *The Kingsbury Gazette* will only be a historic building on Third Avenue."

How is it possible that an institution can break so quickly? Jordan wonders. *And when it's gone, what happens then?*

"Next week?" Jordan asks.

"We've been running in the red for longer than I'd like," Doug confesses. "I would sell the business, but I'd feel guilty selling something that's not worth anything."

Despite Doug's strength in the moment, Jordan can see that the old man who spent a career digging for the truth and bravely sharing it with the citizens of Kingsbury is wounded by this decision.

"It's worth something," Jordan says to him.

Doug laughs. "Probably the land, *maybe* the building. She's got very old bones," he says. "How is your remodeling project coming, by the way?"

Jordan sighs. When he came back to town, he occupied his mind by writing for the *Gazette*, and he occupied his hands by renovating the small fixer-upper his brother bought but never fixed up. Despite moving home, Jordan felt it was too much to also move back into his childhood bedroom. Instead, he landed at Tom's vacant house and couldn't help but fix little things to make it livable—even though it was unclear who would inherit the place.

Of course, all of Tom's plans seem to be coming to light now, Jordan thinks.

"It's a money pit," Jordan says. "I shouldn't be putting anything into it, especially now that whoever wins the treasure hunt is going to get it." He shrugs. "But at least it's a hobby. And I'm learning a lot."

"Reminds me of this place," Doug says. "I've put it through a couple renovations through the years."

"Will you miss it?" Jordan asks.

"It's home, so of course I'll miss it. But I've been here fifty years—thirty as publisher. It's helped me live out a dream career. Sometimes you just have to appreciate what was and let it go," Doug sighs. "How about you? What are you going to do now?"

Jordan shakes his head. "I have no clue," he says. "But it sounds like I'm going to have to figure it out, now that you're firing me."

"Oh, you're not being fired," Doug says. "Your position is being eliminated."

Jordan laughs. "Potato, potahto," he says. "And what about the final issue?"

"What about it?" Doug says.

"What do you have planned for it? Do you have an assignment for me?" Jordan asks.

"It'll have to be something special. A kind of grand finale, I suppose," Doug says. "Do you have something to pitch?"

"I mean, off the top of my head..." Jordan says. "The obvious thing would be a retrospective of the *Gazette* from beginning to end. 'Putting the Paper to Bed after 120 years'."

"It's 119 years," Doug says. "But I like it."

Jordan grins. "Of course," he says, "it would be more meaningful coming from you."

"I'm too cynical for a retrospective," Doug says. "What we really need is the rose-colored hand of someone who grew up thinking *The Kingsbury Gazette* always was and always will be. So will you write it?"

"I would be honored," Jordan says. "I obviously don't have the institutional knowledge you do. I would need to do some research."

"All the better," Doug says. "In fact, I like the idea that you'd be pulling from the pages themselves. 'The proof is in the pudding.' You'll have full access to the archives."

Doug swivels back to his work, his sign that the conversation—while never done—is paused for now.

Jordan slips out of Doug's office and out into the December air.

Great, Jordan thinks. *No job, no prospects, and a ticking time bomb tied to his dwindling bank account.*

As a brisk breeze picks up, Jordan reaches into his work bag to find his gloves. But instead, he finds the half-sheet paper with the treasure hunt rules. And maybe a way to buy himself more time.

TUESDAY, DECEMBER 20

Suzy yanks open the door of Tom's Café at four o'clock in the morning, and she's surprised how easy it is to fall back into her early morning routine.

She remembers how her mom once said coffee shop hours would translate well to her working night shift as a nurse, but she shoves the thought away immediately. Instead, she just enjoys the vacant streets of Kingsbury in early morning as she locks the door behind her and brings Tom's Café to life for another day.

Now that word's gotten out about her being back, Suzy knows the week leading up to Christmas will be some of the busiest, especially with a heightened stock of baked goods in their display cases. And it absolutely warms Suzy's heart. She knows she might become jaded someday about the demands of the work, but right now she's just enjoying the therapy of making something sweet and buttery and having people break their diets to indulge in her creations.

Suzy stashes a few items in her dad's office. And as she turns to leave, she sees a glint of golden wrapping paper on the edge of the desk. "What in the…" she says, picking up a wrapped gift to inspect its attached card.

After the carolers, two additional gifts found their way to Suzy before Monday ended. During her run to the grocery store after work, a stockboy stopped her in the baking aisle to give her a flat item wrapped in golden wrapping paper. "What's this?" she asked him.

"You're Suzy Bell, right?" the guy asked.

"Yeah," Suzy confirmed.

"I was just told to give you that," he said.

"By who?" she asked.

The guy just shrugged and pushed his cart down the aisle. The attached card simply said in the same lilting handwriting as her first card, "Merry Christmas, Darling". When she unwrapped it, Suzy found a vinyl copy of The Carpenters' *Christmas Portrait*.

Then when she got home, Suzy found a golden package containing a box set of *Gilmore Girls*—all seven seasons, plus *A Year in the Life*. The same handwriting on an attached card said, "I smell snow".

And sure, they are spectacular gifts, but they aren't random. *Christmas Portrait*, with Karen's vocals and Richard's arrangements, basically *is* Christmas to Suzy. And if there was such a place, Suzy would move to Stars Hollow in a heartbeat.

She isn't sure whether to be freaked out or flattered that somebody knows her so well.

In her dad's office, Suzy flips open the golden card and reads, "'The tree house started to spin'."

"What on earth," Suzy says. She pulls the wrapping paper back, and she's holding a copy of *Magic Tree House: Tonight on the Titanic* by Mary Pope Osborne.

It's the very first chapter book she couldn't put down. She remembers devouring it like her third-grade life depended on it.

"Almost *no one* knows that," she says in disbelief.

"What was that, hon?" her mom's voice echoes from the front of the shop.

"Did someone stop by after I left yesterday?" Suzy asks.

Her mom stops in the office and hangs up her bag. "No, it was just me and dad. Why?"

She shows her mom the book.

Her mom cocks her head. "*Magic Tree House*," she beams in realization. "You loved those books. That Michael sure knows you well."

"But that's the thing," Suzy says. "He says it isn't him."

"Maybe he's just trying keep up the suspense," Suzy's mom says.

"Or maybe," Suzy says, "I have a stalker."

Her mom laughs. "A stalker that sends you a series of customized, sentimental birthday gifts?"

Her mom walks into the kitchen and pulls on an apron.

"These are *not* birthday gifts," Suzy says, following her mom. "There's a big difference, and these are Christmas gifts."

"Suze…" her mom says.

"Carolers and *Christmas Portrait*?" Suzy says, as if making her closing arguments in front of a grand jury.

"And *Gilmore Girls*?" her mom asks.

"It has Christmas episodes," Suzy justifies.

"They're wrapped in golden paper," her mom says.

"Gold is a Christmas thing too," Suzy argues.

"Oh, Suze," her mom says as she wraps her daughter in a hug and chuckles. "I think the fact that he—or she—promised twenty-three gifts for your twenty-third *golden* birthday is proof that they're *birthday* gifts."

"And I think," Suzy says, "if this person really knew me, they would know I don't like to conflate my birthday and Christmas."

Suzy's mom pulls back from her daughter to look her in the face. "Either way," she says, "you really shouldn't look a gift horse in the mouth. Maybe just appreciate the gesture."

Suzy thinks about this for a moment.

"Is it you and dad?" Suzy asks.

Suzy's mom laughs. "I definitely had nothing to do with it," she says. "And if your dad did, he's been doing a lot of running around buying things with cash, because I didn't see any of these on the credit card statements." Her mom rubs Suzy's back and gives it a pat before setting off to do her store-opening chores. "So what are we baking today?"

"Mm," Suzy thinks. "I've been wanting to make butterscotch bars. And there's this recipe for cardamom scones I want to try."

"Sounds amazing," her mom says.

"Christmas flavors," Suzy shrugs.

"You mean *birthday* flavors," her mom winks.

Suzy crosses her arms. "You're not funny."

"I'm *kidding*," her mom says. "You put your book away, and I'll heat the ovens."

As she stashes *Tonight on the Titanic* in her dad's office, Suzy takes another look at the lilting handwriting on the card. She could swear she's seen it before. It feels almost as nostalgic as *Christmas Portrait* and *Gilmore Girls* and *Night on the Titanic*. But she just can't put her finger on it.

***

Call it a sixth sense, but Suzy feels another gift coming her way when the delivery man pulls up at ten o'clock. And sure enough, he hands her a stack of mail accompanied by a small golden box addressed to "Suzy Bell, c/o Tom's Café".

She walks the mail to her dad's office, gives him a stack of envelopes, and places the box on his desk.

"I need you to stand by just in case this package is laced with anthrax or something," Suzy says to her dad.

"Is that another birthday gift?" he says, standing up. "I have to tell you, this is very fun for me."

Suzy grabs a pair of scissors to slice open the package. "I'm so happy you're being entertained," she says with sarcasm, and she cuts the tape along the box's sealed seams.

Suzy pulls out bubble wrap and fishes out another card, with the same handwriting.

"'Don't be afraid'," she reads.

She turns to her dad. "Do you see what I'm saying now?" she asks. "That is *creepy*, dad."

"Okay, yeah. But what's the gift?" he asks.

"Just wait a second," Suzy says, passing him the card. "Do you recognize this handwriting?"

Her dad puts on his reading glasses and takes a close look. "No idea," he says.

Suzy reaches into the box, and—

"Ah!" her dad yells.

Suzy screams.

She smacks him on the arm. "Don't do that!" she says. "I'm already freaked out enough."

She reaches in her hand and feels fur. She pushes the box away and says, "No, I can't. It's some kind of dead animal or something."

"Oh, please," her dad says, picking up the box.

He reaches in and pulls out some kind of striped furry rodent—or something—attached by its nose to a color-blocked plastic ball.

"Ha!" her dad says and pretends to throw it right at her.

"NO!" Suzy shrieks. "What *is* that?!"

"What's happening back here?" her mom says from the doorway.

"You don't remember when you got a Weazel Ball for your third birthday?" Suzy's dad says.

"I was *three*," Suzy says. "How would I remember that?"

"You put batteries in the ball, and it flops around uncontrollably?" her dad says. "You were traumatized by the thing, and it was *so* funny."

"That's right," her mom says, reaching out to touch the furry thing. "I think it's supposed to be a cat toy."

"What a blast from the past!" her dad grins.

"But who would know about that?" Suzy says.

Her dad laughs. "Probably anybody we knew when it happened," he says. "We carried the thing around with us for about a month and told everybody the story."

Suzy crosses her arms. "So that's not helpful," she says.

Her dad pulls one of his desk drawers open and starts pushing things aside.

"What are you doing?" Suzy asks.

"Trying to find some batteries," her dad says. "I wanna see it in action again."

"Ugh," Suzy sighs as she storms back to the front of the shop. *I'm going to figure out who this terrorist gift giver is, even if it's the last thing I do.*

Seven

Kara barely drops her work bag onto her desk before Wendy seemingly appears out of thin air.

"So how was it?" Wendy asks.

Kara gives Wendy a withering stare. "How was it?" she says. "You stood me up."

"No," Wendy says. "I had a substitute fill in for me. Ipso facto, you're welcome."

Kara frowns and goes about setting up her workstation for the day.

"You at least have to admit he's cute," Wendy says.

"What I admit is that you lured me there under false pretenses," Kara says.

"Or at least that he's nice," Wendy says.

"Fine," Kara says, sitting down on her desk chair. "He's cute and he's nice and he did a great job renovating the old Rainbow Ice Cream. Is that what you want to hear?"

"In fact," Wendy smiles, "it is. So are you going to see him again?"

Kara rolls her eyes. "So the thing is," she says, "Frank Amundson was at the restaurant, and I kind of got into a very public argument with him about the Christmas Festival."

Wendy thinks about it for a second, trying to fit the pieces together. "Okay?" Wendy says.

"I'm proud that I stood up for myself," Kara says.

"Amazing," Wendy says.

"I'm not as proud," continues Kara, "of how it may have looked to a complete stranger."

"It couldn't have been that bad," Wendy says.

"Brent asked if me and Frank wanted to continue our conversation in the restaurant side room," Kara says. "I think that means it was pretty disruptive and bad."

Wendy winces. "It's a good thing that first impressions aren't all that important?" Wendy tries.

"No one has ever said that," Kara huffs.

"It's a small town. Maybe if you keep crossing paths, he'll get to see the amazing person you are," Wendy says to comfort her friend.

"What gave you the idea to set me up like that anyway?" Kara asks.

"Me and Greg tried out The Wheelhouse over the weekend," Wendy says. "And *I* don't know… I asked if Brent was single, and I said I had a friend who was also single, and—"

"You really can't help yourself," Kara says.

"I have a problem, okay," Wendy says. "But you're too good to just be sitting on the shelf. It's time to make a life for yourself."

"I have a life," Kara says.

"I know you do," Wendy says. "I guess what I'm trying to say is, do you want to share it with someone?"

Kara takes a deep breath. "Yes, I would," she admits.

"So you've gotta kiss a couple frogs," Wendy says. "Not that Brent is a frog. But ribbit-ribbit, Lord knows I kissed a few before I found Greg."

As Kara's boss Will walks in the door, Wendy pats Suzy's desk. "I better get to work," she says, scooting off to her cubicle.

"Morning!" Will says to Kara. "Say, can I see you in my office quick?"

"Sure," Kara says.

Kara waits a beat while Will settles in, then she grabs a notepad and a pen. Even though she knows her boss calling her into his office right when he walks in the door isn't a good sign, she tries to remain calm, collected, zen.

And then there's the little voice in the back of her head saying, *This is it. He's finally figured out you're a fraud and is going to fire you!*

"Open or closed?" Kara asks as she hovers in the office door.

"Uh, closed," Will says as he sits down on his desk chair. "And take a seat."

Kara closes the door behind her and sits at the small circular worktable in Will's office. As the school district's business manager, Will could have an office stacked with papers, but he keeps a tight ship. Kara still doesn't know if neatnik behavior is an indicator of a good boss or not. But she's worked with Will for three years without major crisis, so maybe a stable environment is all she could ask for.

"You're not in trouble," Will says. "I just want to know more about a conversation you had with Frank Amundson yesterday at that new restaurant in town."

"Yes," Kara says. "The Wheelhouse."

"That's the one," Will says.

Kara swallows. "As you know," she says, "I'm working with Frank on planning the Christmas Festival this Friday.

Unfortunately, my vision and Frank's vision for the event haven't... we haven't seen eye to eye."

"Okay," Will says.

"Yesterday at the restaurant I overheard him talking about how he thought I was doing a poor job and that my brother Tom, who helped organize the Festival previously, also did a poor job. And I felt forced to confront him," Kara says. "He threw some accusations at me and then resigned from the Festival committee."

Will nods. "So," he says, "the reality of working for the school district—especially working with public money like we do in our positions—is that the nature of our jobs is political, whether we like it or not. Frank has a lot of power in Kingsbury, and as you know, his wife Georgia is on the school board."

"Yes," Kara says in acknowledgement.

"Someone told the superintendent about your exchange with Frank," Will says. "And like I said, you're not in trouble. But I was asked to issue a word of caution when crossing paths with Frank and Georgia Amundson. Do you understand?"

"Yes," Kara says. "I can honestly say that I'm starting to regret getting involved with the Christmas Festival at all."

"I think it's good that you're involved in the community," Will says. "I just think being involved in small town drama isn't helpful to our success here in the office."

"I completely understand," Kara assures him.

"Good," Will says. "Thanks for talking this through with me."

Kara stands and opens the door. "Open or closed?" she asks Will on her way out.

"Open," he says. "Thanks, Kara."

***

Kara works through lunch so she can escape for an hour in the afternoon to run errands for the Festival.

Her first stop is the local hardware store, where she had to place a special order for string lights with a certain temperature and energy rating—*who knew?!*

She walks straight up to the counter at Kingsbury Tool and Supply and tells the clerk she's picking up a special order of lights.

"Oh," the clerk says, "your order was actually already picked up this morning."

"What?" Kara says. "There must be a mistake. I'm the one who placed the order. I mean, it was thirty sets of very specific string lights."

The clerk looks at the transaction records. "I see that here," he says. "And it was ordered through the Kingsbury Community Club's account."

"That's correct," Kara says.

"But it was paid for by," the clerk takes a closer look at the record, "Frank Amundson. And that makes sense, since I saw him here this morning."

"Okay," Kara says, still trying to be optimistic this can be fixed. "But Frank wasn't the one who ordered them."

"Yes," the clerk says, "but it's his name on the Community Club account. Maybe you could reach out to him and ask?"

"Maybe," Kara says, not wanting to deal with Frank if at all possible. "By chance, do you have any of those same lights in stock?"

"Let me check," the clerk says, searching through the inventory system. After a moment, he says, "I'm sorry, no. We have other string lights, but I'm afraid nowhere close to that quantity."

Kara sighs. "If I wanted to take a look, what aisle would they be in?"

"Aisle three," the clerk says. "I'm sorry again."

Is that even legal? Kara asks herself as she walks to aisle three. *Taking someone else's order?!*

She finds the section with the string lights, but the clerk was right. The stock is especially low, which doesn't surprise Kara when it's the week before Christmas.

"You have to be kidding me," Kara says.

She takes a deep breath and considers that the Festival will be just fine without the extra lights in Carlson Square.

She decides to move on.

Kara finds herself across the street at the dental office, where she's been getting her teeth treated her entire life. The place smells like oxygenated air and mint.

"Kara!" the receptionist Sharon says as she walks in. "It's so good to see you. What brings you in today?"

"Hey, Sharon," Kara smiles. "Just going around town to confirm that you're still on for tabling at the Christmas Festival on Friday."

For the past few years, Kingsbury Dental has been part of a series of kid-centered stations where people collect all the ingredients for hot cocoa and then combine everything together. The dentist always oversees giving out the mini marshmallows, which they brand as "snowman teeth". Personally, the idea of snowmen having teeth rubs Kara the wrong way, but she thinks most things involving kids are a bit odd and creepy. Also, Kara feels that a dentist giving out candy maybe goes against their brand, but whatever.

Sharon's face goes blank. "Didn't you get the memo?" she asks.

Kara's stomach drops, but she tries to stay upbeat. "I must not have!" she says.

"It's so sad. The Festival is canceled," Sharon says. "I guess something happened with Frank, and he's not able to do it this year."

What?! Kara thinks.

Kara stifles a laugh. "I was actually co-chairing the Festival planning committee with Frank. It's true that he dropped out, but the Festival is still going on."

"That's not the word going around town," Sharon says.

Kara tries to smile, but she's afraid her wide eyes are making her look more crazed than joyful.

"I'm sorry," Sharon says.

"No worries," Kara says. "And thank you for letting me know, Sharon. I'll get this all straightened out. But please continue to plan for Friday, okay?"

"Sounds wonderful!" Sharon says.

As soon as Kara steps out onto the sidewalk, she can't help but let out a kind of primal scream and starts kicking a snowbank out of fury.

She momentarily feels much better until she looks up and sees Brent staring at her about thirty feet away, with a look of concern on his face.

"Are you okay?" he asks.

"I'm fine," Kara says, face flushed with embarrassment. She walks away and thinks, *Dear God, why?*

Eight

Jordan arrives to Carlson Square just before five o'clock, and a crowd of about fifty people is already assembled for the reveal of the treasure hunt's second clue.

Considering his brother's quarter-million-dollar estate is on the line, Jordan's not surprised by the turnout. But what *does* surprise him is how many people he doesn't recognize. He knows word travels fast, but seeing it draw an in-person crowd is something else entirely. And now he sees at least three separate TV journalists setting up cameras on the edge of the Square. He can imagine the treasure hunt becoming even more contentious after this evening's news.

Jordan takes a deep breath of cold air as a blast of orchestral music sounds, quieting the crowd. But it quickly fades to silence as two dozen ballerinas take their places on the periphery of the Square.

From the ranks, one ballerina takes position in the middle of the Square, where a dance floor has been installed. And when the sound of a stringed instrument starts a familiar plucking, the ballerina starts dancing to "Dance of the Sugar Plum Fairy".

After a couple minutes, the ballerinas on the edges of the Square filter through the crowd from all sides to join the lead dancer. They all dance in unison for a swirl of tutus and synchronized limbs to close out the performance.

Applause erupts as the ballerinas bow, and a second large banner unfurls with a thrush of a harp and the second clue:

> I've traversed the map;
> I've scoured the edges.
> I've punched through the paper,
> Found nothing but ledges.
> Imagine my shock
> When all of my questions
> All could be answered
> With Kingsbury legends.

Kingsbury legends? Jordan thinks.

The crowd erupts into its pre-ballet chatter. Some groups of treasure hunters go running, presumably thinking that the treasure's location is obvious and that it's now just a matter of who gets there first. Others huddle together in hushed whispers, trying to conceal their scheming.

Jordan looks across the Square and spots Beatrice, looking over the bustle of the crowd with her jaw set and her mouth in a thin line.

Jordan walks toward Beatrice with a smile.

"Hey," he says when he's in earshot.

Her face seems to soften as she sees him. "Hey," she says, trying to muster a smile but having it not quite reach her eyes.

"Quite a show," Jordan says.

"Your brother," she says in return, "had *very* specific instructions."

Jordan looks at the ground. "It does all feel very *him*," he says, looking up to see Beatrice staring at him before she quickly looks away.

A section of hair falls in front of her face. His initial reaction is to sweep it behind her ear, but he stops himself.

"He loved a spectacle," Beatrice says, pushing the hair back herself. "But I wonder if he intended such a large audience."

Jordan scoffs. "A choir of children and the Sugar Plum Fairy? Oh, Tom wanted an audience," he says.

Beatrice smiles and pauses as if she has more to say. But instead, she starts to walk away.

"So…" Tom says, following her. "'Kingsbury legends'?"

"Kingsbury legends," Beatrice confirms. "Do you know what it means?"

"I mean, maybe," Jordan says. "Maps, edges… Questions, answers… It sounds like historical research."

"Hm," Beatrice nods.

"Specifically, Kingsbury history?" Jordan fishes.

She shrugs. "It sounds like a good lead. And you may have a leg up, having access to *The Kingsbury Gazette* archives and all."

Jordan didn't think of that…

"I'm writing a history retrospective of the *Gazette*," Jordan says.

"Oh," Beatrice says, "that seems appropriate for the last issue."

Jordan is surprised she knows about the *Gazette* being closed by the end of the year. "How did you hear?"

"I ran into Doug at the Post Office," Beatrice says. "It's sad to see it go, but he did his best to keep it alive." She winces. "I guess that means you're losing your job, huh?"

Jordan breathes deeply. "Yeah," he confirms.

"And you're leaving town again?" Beatrice asks.

Jordan stops in his tracks, and Beatrice holds back too. "I'm trying to figure that out," he says. "Maybe if I win Tom's estate, I can stick around a little longer."

Beatrice smiles, "It'd be nice to see you stay. But... I don't think you should waste your time on the treasure hunt."

"What?" Jordan asks. "Why not?"

"Well," she says, "how would it look if Tom's brother won the thing? Maybe somebody else is meant to win."

"I'm not passing up my chance to win Tom's estate," Jordan says. "I live in his house."

"I can't blame you there," she says, continuing to walk and leaving Jordan behind. "Good luck wading through a hundred years of newspapers," she says over her shoulder.

***

Jordan pores through back issues of *The Kingsbury Gazette* for an hour or so, his mind swimming with Tom's first two clues.

He starts to wonder if the clues mean anything at all—or if they only mean something in the context of knowing Tom himself.

Obviously, Tom would want his estate to go to someone who knew him well, Jordan reasons. *What part of Kingsbury history was closest to Tom?*

Jordan didn't see or talk to his brother often over the past few years. Truth be told, they didn't share many of the same interests and had a few disagreements along the way that kept them apart. But Jordan knew all about Tom's life. Tom helped plan the Christmas Festival every year and, by extension, also served on the Community Club board. He loved art and volunteered with different arts programs—music, theatre, film club—at the high school. And he held a special place in his heart for baseball, calling high school games from the sound booth behind home plate.

But maybe the most relevant piece of the puzzle was Tom's work with the Kingsbury Historical Society. When Tom died, he was president of the Historical Society. And alongside his girlfriend Jessica, he had spent the past few years saving an old railroad building from demolition and renovating it to become a historical museum.

Why didn't I think of it before? Jordan asks himself.

Jordan heads directly across town to the Kingsbury Historical Museum.

When he pulls open the door, Jordan hears a digital *ping* echo through the building. He cranes his neck around at the black and white photos of Kingsbury's history lining the walls—women bowling in a basement, thousands of people crowding the stands at a baseball field, a main street flooded with water up over the hoods of classic cars.

The pictures represent a Kingsbury Jordan doesn't know—and Tom spent years trying to understand. *Imagine all the stories this town has*, Jordan thinks.

"Welcome!" says an older woman from behind the reception desk. "Now *you* have to be Tom Bell's brother."

The woman seems familiar to Jordan, like he's spent years seeing her around town but never formally met her.

He smiles and extends his hand to shake hers. "Yes," he says, "I'm Jordan, Tom's younger brother."

The woman folds both of her hands around Jordan's extended hand. "I'm Marianne Joki," she says. "You are the spitting image of Tom. When you walked through the door, I thought you were a ghost!"

Jordan doesn't feel like Tom and him looked all that alike, but the number of times he's heard this sentiment—especially since Tom's passing—makes Jordan think he may be wrong.

"You could have been twins!" Marianne muses. "So handsome and tall. It was a shame we lost him so young."

"Thank you," Jordan says, unsure exactly how to respond to Marianne's enthusiasm.

"What brings you in today?" Marianne asks.

"I've never been here," Jordan says. "I'm actually doing that treasure hunt that's going on?"

"Sure," she says, "I've seen a few people come through here today about that. What questions do you have about Kingsbury's 'legends'?" she asks with a wink.

"I'm not sure," Jordan says, thinking back to the clue. "Do you have maps or any information about ledges or… shocks? I'm not sure what I should be looking for, to be honest."

Marianne smiles. "I could talk about all those things. We sure have maps—a stack of drawers with hundreds of them. And ledges could go a lot of ways. There are a couple rock formations in town that could be classified that way, but nothing of significance there. The closest to a shock I can think of is the 'Kingsbury Flicker', which is what the locals called the way the power came and went while the railroad ran the utilities in town."

"Huh," Jordan says. "Where do you think I should start?"

Marianne holds up her finger with an idea. "Follow me," she says, keeping her finger up as she leads Jordan to a door. "The archive room," she announces, pushing open the door. "Everything you could ever want to know about Kingsbury in one place."

I am so going to win that treasure hunt, Jordan thinks.

WEDNESDAY, DECEMBER 21

Nine

Suzy and Mike sit at a table in Tom's Café, trying to organize her investigation. "Okay," she says, "the gift giver is not my mom, not my dad, not my gran, not my siblings, not you—"

"Wait," Mike says from across the table. "When did you rule out Kara and Jordan?"

Suzy shrugs. "Since I just know it's not them," she says.

"Some of these gifts are from when you were a kid," Mike says. "They should stay on the list until you can say for sure it's not them."

Suzy shakes her head. "Those two are too self-involved," she says. "I never even see them."

"But they have access to the shop, to your parents' house," Mike says. "You can't dismiss that."

"We should really focus our attention elsewhere," Suzy says.

"Let's run down the list of gifts again," Mike suggests. "Maybe we're missing something."

"Okay," Suzy says, flipping her paper over to her list of gifts received. "Monday was the carolers, Carpenters, *Gilmore Girls*. Tuesday was Magic Tree House, weasel, Tremblay's fudge, massage, Taylor Swift cardigan. And Wednesday so far has been my own ice skates being newly sharpened."

"See," Mike says, "that's what I'm saying. Whoever's doing all this not only has access to your house, but also knows where you store your skates. Are you sure your parents aren't in on it? Your brother and sister?"

"At this point," Suzy sighs, "I think *many* people are in on it. They're just sworn to secrecy or signed an NDA or something. Maybe that's the true gift in all of this—the realization that everybody's a *liar*. Really helps set expectations for the rest of life."

"Well, *I'm* not lying to you," Mike says. "I have absolutely no knowledge of this whole thing whatsoever." He sticks his hand in the air. "Scout's honor."

"You are not a Boy Scout," Suzy says.

"Well, I *was!*" Mike says. "And I was," he holds up his index finger and thumb an inch apart, *"this close* to an Eagle Scout."

Suzy is not amused at one of Mike's standard jokes. "And then what happened?" she asks deadpan.

"The Eagle Scout got up and moved chairs," Mike says.

"Anyway," Suzy says, flipping her paper back over, "who else do we need to add to this list? And remember, to pull this whole thing off they'd have to be local—or have an army of local people to do their bidding."

"Other relatives?" Mike asks.

"All live out of town," Suzy says.

"Friends from high school?" Mike says.

"Maybe," she says. "Except I haven't really connected with Erin or Chloe since the summer after graduation."

"Friends from college?" a voice carries from the shop's front door.

Suzy turns around to see the source of the voice, and it takes her a second to place the man standing there.

"Paul? What on earth?!" she says, jumping up to run and give him a hug.

Suzy met Paul Carey at her first year of nursing school in the Cities. When they found out they shared the same list of classes, they quickly connected as study buddies—and stayed that way ever since.

"What are you doing here?" Suzy says.

"Yeah," Mike says, coming up behind Suzy. "What are you doing here?"

Suzy notices a bit of jealousy in Mike. But Paul sidesteps any tension with a laugh and a good-natured handshake with Mike. "It's good to see you, Mike. Can we sit down?"

"Of course," Suzy says, leading him back to their table.

"It was the craziest thing," Paul says. "I finished my last final yesterday, and when I got home there was a card waiting at my door."

He pulls out a golden envelope with "Paul" scrawled on it in the same lilting handwriting as the cards from her gifts. He hands it to Suzy, and she opens it.

"'Paul, I need your help,'" Suzy reads. "'We are celebrating Suzy's golden birthday this week in Kingsbury, and it would be a fantastic surprise for you to join Suzy for the festivities. Please arrive at Tom's Café between ten and eleven o'clock on Wednesday. Plan to stay through her birthday on Friday. And don't tell Suzy—it's a surprise!'"

"I guess that settles whether these are Christmas gifts or birthday gifts," Mike says.

This confirmation brings Suzy no satisfaction, though Mike pointing it out brings irritation. "I guess," Suzy says, "but it's still strange."

"Oh," Paul says, pulling out another golden card. "And I think I'm supposed to give you this."

Paul hands Suzy the same type of golden card from her other gifts, again with the same lilting handwriting.

"'You've got a friend'," she reads.

Suzy takes a moment to inspect the handwriting on Paul's first card to see if she can spot any clues to the gift giver. Her other cards didn't have this amount of text, and she now notices how exact the handwriting is, how perfect each letter is formed. There isn't any spontaneity, each letter and line uniform and perfectly spaced.

It's clear now that it's not handwriting—it's a font.

Was the handwriting of someone I know turned into a font? she wonders.

If that's the case, the uniformity of the text seems to block Suzy from recognizing the handwriting.

"And they weren't even put through the mail," Paul says. "They were just leaning up against my door. So of course I had to come check out what this was all about."

Suzy lays down the cards on the table. "Some mystery person has apparently arranged twenty-three presents for me," Suzy explains, showing him the paper listing her gifts. "I've been getting them since I got into town on Monday. Mike and I were just trying to brainstorm who it could be."

"Huh," Paul says. "Any ideas?"

"Nothing concrete," Suzy says.

"Wait," Mike says. "Paul, didn't you just say your last final was yesterday?"

"Yeah," Paul nods.

Mike looks at Suzy. "I thought you were both in all the same classes?" he asks.

Suzy's eyes go wide. "I—uh, took it early so I could get home sooner," Suzy lies.

Paul looks at her like she just sprouted a second nose.

"It was a hard one, wasn't it?" Suzy says to Paul.

Confused, Paul says, "I didn't think it was too bad."

"Anyway, we should add you to the gift list," Suzy says, scrawling "Paul" as number ten on her list. "Can I get you something to drink?" Suzy asks Paul, standing up abruptly.

"I could use a black coffee to go," Mike says.

Suzy looks at Mike, not having expected him to answer.

"I need to get back to work," Mike says to Paul.

"Yeah, it's too bad," Suzy says. "And for you, Paul?"

Paul nods, "I'm good with black coffee too."

***

Suzy sends Mike on his way and shares the news about Paul's arrival with her mom, who insists the friends take a walk to catch up.

"What was all that about you taking the final early?" Paul asks.

Suzy sighs. "I haven't exactly gotten around to telling people about dropping out of school," she says.

"Not even Mike?" Paul says.

Suzy feels her cheeks burn in embarrassment. "I know it's stupid," she says. "I just feel like if anyone knows about it, word will get back to my parents."

"Why not get ahead of it then?" Paul asks. "Just tell everybody and get it over with. Start with your parents."

"I…" Suzy trails off. "I sometimes wonder if it was a really stupid thing to do—dropping out."

"Stupid is one word for it," Paul says. "But if you stand in your conviction and wear it proudly, another word would be brave."

Suzy considers this.

"But having that label," Paul says, "would actually require you to be brave and tell people about it."

Ouch, Suzy thinks.

"I'm trying to," she says. "It's just that I'm afraid what my parents will say. They're *so* proud of their daughter going to school to become a nurse. And it was easy to be bold about it when I was back in the Cities. But then I came home, and Tom's memory seems so fresh. And it's kind of like I was following in his footsteps by going into healthcare."

"I get that it's complex," Paul says. "But do you really think Tom would have wanted you to tiptoe around and lie to your parents for days on end? I never met the guy, but he sure seems like the type to just say what he means and mean what he says."

Suzy sighs again. "Can you just keep it between me and you until I'm ready to share?" she asks.

"You can't possibly ask me to lie for you," Paul says.

"You're exhausting," Suzy says.

"Maybe that's the reason I was included in this whole golden gift thing," he smiles. "The real gift was somebody coming to talk some sense into you!"

Ten

Kara writes her name on the sign-in sheet and enters the City Council chambers with five minutes to spare. At the front of the room, the Councilors and city staff bustle about their u-shaped dais, and a few spectators like Kara find a perch within the audience of mostly empty stackable chairs.

Frank is among the few non-city personnel there. He nods in Kara's direction before she sits, and it takes everything in her to keep things polite, returning only with a smirk and head nod.

Kara thumbs through the agenda she picked up at the sign-in table. She knows she isn't staying for the entire meeting, but she figures she ought to know what else is on the agenda before she updates the Council that, yes, the Festival *is* still happening. And yes, it *will* be successful, despite some people's best efforts to thwart it.

She would like to really call out Frank on the carpet. *But we're keeping it classy for Tom,* Kara thinks.

Dottie huffs through the door, aided by her cane. Kara waves at her, and Dottie works her way over and takes a load off on the seat next to Kara.

"The sidewalk is basically a skating rink," Dottie says. "Did you manage all right out there?"

Kara laughs and says, "I just tried to follow the salt and sand."

"A wise woman," Dottie nods.

From the front of the room, the mayor calls the meeting to order, and the room stands for the pledge of allegiance. The Council goes quickly through roll call attendance, a vote to approve the minutes from the previous meeting, and a vote to approve the meeting agenda before turning to those in the audience. The mayor says, "We set aside time during each meeting to hear comments and suggestions from citizens present. If you would like to speak, please queue up at the microphone."

There's an older woman who complains about the City plow creating banks of snow at the end of her driveway. Then a man in his fifties goes to the microphone to share concern about the accumulation of "junk cars" his neighbors have sitting on their property. He slaps the lectern with his hand. "*When* will the blight ordinance be enforced?" he demands. The Council just stares at him until he throws his hands in the air and leaves the Council chambers.

Kara looks around and, with no one else making a move, jumps up to stand behind the lectern—and the microphone.

"Good evening, Mr. Mayor and members of the Council," she starts.

"Will you state your name and address for the record?" the mayor asks.

"Yes," Kara says. "Kara Bell. 624 Slosson Street. I'm visiting tonight to once again extend an invite to the entire community for the Christmas Festival, this Friday in Carlson Square from five to nine in the evening. There's going to be—"

"Excuse me," the mayor interrupts.

"Oh, sorry," Kara stops. "Do you have a question?"

The mayor tilts his head and looks past Kara into the crowd, right where Frank is sitting. "Did you not tell her?" he asks.

Kara looks behind her to see Frank shake his head.

"Oh geez," the mayor says. "Kara, I'm sorry to have to be the one to share this with you."

Kara looks at Frank again and back to the mayor. "Share what?" she asks.

"Well," the mayor says, "the Council received word from some of the businesses and—more importantly—the Community Club that planning for the Festival wasn't going well. The Community Club was the organization that applied for event permits with the City, and so we talked to Mr. Amundson as the Club's representative."

Kara looks behind her to see Frank looking straight ahead, arms crossed over his chest. Without looking away, she says, "And what did Mr. Amundson say?"

"Mr. Amundson withdrew the permit application," the mayor says.

It's like a swift kick to Kara's gut. In fact, it's so swift Kara doesn't even believe what she's just heard.

"Despite Mr. Amundson," Kara says, "the Festival is proceeding full steam ahead at Carlson Square on Friday at—"

"I'm afraid you don't understand," the mayor interjects again. "If the Community Club pulls its application, the City pulls its permits. And if the City—"

"The City Council already approved the permits," Kara reminds the elected officials.

"And if the City pulls its permits, there is no Festival," the mayor concludes. "Part of tonight's consent agenda, which the Council is ready to vote in favor of without further discussion, is declining permission to use the Square on Friday night."

Kara is speechless.

"Now," the mayor continues, "you are free to hold a private gathering elsewhere on Friday, but I'm afraid the Community Club would not cover liability for that event. Is that right, Frank?"

Frank clears his throat. "That's correct," he says.

The mayor nods. "So if the Festival is to be held under your direction, Miss Bell, it would need to be organized and hosted privately by you."

Kara steps back from the microphone for a minute and faces Frank.

How dare he?! she thinks. *After all of the planning, all of the organizing I had to singlehandedly do because neither he nor anyone else could bother to lift a finger, he pulls this?!*

Kara steps back up to the microphone. "How about a protest in Carlson Square?" she says, unable to keep her voice from shaking. "How about I gather every *single* person I know, and we protest the City of Kingsbury, the Community Club, and Mr. Frank Amundson himself for the disservice he brings to this town every day he lives and breathes?"

"Well," the mayor says, "I wouldn't—"

"Wouldn't what?" Kara asks. "Want to impede my constitutional right to a peaceful protest? I agree that it wouldn't be wise." Kara swivels around to look at Frank and says directly into the microphone, "What do you think of that, Frank?"

Frank simply smirks and nods at Kara, which only boils her blood more.

"Kara," the mayor says, "no one is stopping you from holding a gathering at a private establishment, open to the public, and calling it the Christmas Festival."

"Do you think I have a private establishment to invite the public to?" Kara flings back at the mayor. "Do you think I wanted to do any of this to begin with?" Kara can feel herself becoming unhinged, but it's like she's hovering outside of her body and forced to watch herself unravel in a very public way. "You know, *everybody* talks about how *nobody* wants to step up and volunteer and make things better in this town. Well, *this* is the reason. People like *Frank Amundson* are the reason that this town's community spirit and willingness to lend a hand and even get to know your neighbor is *dying*," Kara spits. She turns to the Council members at the front of the room. "What are you going to do about it, Mr. Mayor and members of the Council? Are you going to just sit by and watch this community *die* while people like *Frank Amundson* hold on too tightly to a beloved community event that everyone will *consider* attending but no one is willing to help put on?"

"Kara," the mayor says, "I know you're disappointed, but if the Community Club doesn't—"

"I'm not 'disappointed'. I am angry that I wasted so much time thinking I could make a difference in this town," she says. "And I'm angry that my brother spent the very little time he had on earth trying to make a difference and having to deal with petty people like *Frank Amundson* to try to do it!" Kara turns to Frank again to deliver her grand finale.

But she feels a hand touch her shoulder.

Kara turns to see Dottie, who slides her hand down Kara's shoulder to gently rub her forearm. "Kara, you've done a good job demonstrating your frustration," Dottie says. "Let's go grab a cup of cocoa."

Kara takes in the warmth in Dottie's eyes. She turns to see Frank's unmoving resolution and then to the mayor and Council to see their concern for the unhinged woman she's become.

How could I be so stupid? Nothing I could say or do will make any difference with any of these people, she thinks.

Kara lays her hand on Dottie's arm in turn, gives her friend a quick nod, and gathers up her bag from her seat before marching out of the Council chambers.

Eleven

Jordan pulls open the door of the Kingsbury Historical Museum as a digital *ping* echoes through the building.

Marianne stands up from her desk with a smile. "You just couldn't stay away!" she says.

Though Jordan did his best to get a lay of the archive room and start poking around yesterday, his time was short since the Museum closed only an hour after he arrived. As time ran out, he decided it would be best to collect his thoughts and return the next day with a game plan of topics to research and explore.

Jordan smiles back. "It sure seems that way," he says. "Has it been busy today?"

"Only as busy as it usually is," Marianne says. "Maybe a few more people in town for the holidays that want something to do."

Good, Jordan thinks. *No huge rush from treasure hunters.*

Jordan thumbs back toward the archive room. "Can I just go on back to the archives then?"

Marianne gives him a look of pity.

"Uh oh," he says. "Is it closed or something?"

Marianne sighs, "Well, our executive director said that if you came—"

"Only to you," Beatrice says from the archive room doorway.

It takes a moment to place Beatrice in this context. "You're the executive director?" he says.

"Yes," Beatrice says, "I am. I take it you didn't find what you were looking for in the *Gazette* back issues?"

"Correct," Jordan says. "So why can't I look at the archives?"

Beatrice closes the archive room door and walks toward Jordan, wrapping her arms around herself. "I told you before. This treasure hunt isn't meant for you," she says.

"The rules say anyone can participate," Jordan says.

"That's true," Beatrice agrees. "But I'm saying you shouldn't waste your time."

"I'm practically jobless and homeless. I have all the time in the world to waste," Jordan says. "Do you *want* to get rid of me or something?"

"I don't want—" Beatrice starts to say, then stops herself. "You know—"

She's flustered. It doesn't happen often. But Jordan secretly loves when it does, and he can't help smiling.

Beatrice takes a breath. "I suppose you're free to do whatever you want," she concludes.

"So I can go back and check out the archives," Jordan says with a grin.

Beatrice purses her lips. "Except that," she says. "The archives are closed to the public today."

"Oh!" Marianne says from behind her reception desk. "To everyone?"

"Just for today," Beatrice says, turning back to the archive room. "There's some cleaning needed before it's presentable for additional guests."

"But didn't you just re-organize everything in there last week?" Marianne asks.

Beatrice turns and stares at Marianne, trying to telepathically tell her, *Work with me!*

When that doesn't seem to wipe the blank expression off Marianne's face, Beatrice says, "Well, unfortunately Mister Bell here left quite a mess after his visit yesterday. I think it will be closed the rest of the week, now that I think about it."

Beatrice smiles at Jordan.

Two can play at this game, he thinks.

Jordan crosses his arms over his chest to mirror her.

"Is the rest of the Museum closed as well?" Jordan asks.

"Of course not," Beatrice says. "You're welcome to take a look around. But just as a warning, you're not going to find what you're looking for."

"How do I know you're not just telling me that?" Jordan says. "Besides, maybe you don't know your own museum as well as you think you do."

"Oh, I assure you," Marianne chimes in, "no one knows this museum as well as Beatrice. She curated every exhibit."

"Is that true?" Jordan asks Beatrice teasingly.

Jordan sees Beatrice's face start to flush.

"Absolutely it is!" Marianne says. "She's very talented with computers and designs all the exhibits herself."

"I don't think—" Beatrice tries to interrupt.

But Marianne is on a mission. "The installation about the women railroaders during World War II downstairs?" she says. "That one actually won an award—"

"Marianne!" Beatrice yells. She covers her mouth and tries to regain her composure. "Jordan's not interested in all that," Beatrice says.

"She's so humble," Marianne says to Jordan with a smile.

"But like I said," Beatrice continues to Jordan, "you're free to look around if you want."

Beatrice opens the archive room door to escape the conversation.

I guess I'll try the Gazette *back issues again*, Jordan thinks.

He turns to head out of the Museum, but then he catches Beatrice peeking back at him before she softly closes the archive room door. And seeing her still flustered, Jordan stops in his tracks. He feels wrong about leaving Beatrice like that. And he feels especially guilty treating her poorly with everything she's doing to carry out her brother's wishes with the treasure hunt.

Jordan takes a deep breath and walks to the archive room door. He closes his eyes and wraps on the door with his knuckle.

Beatrice nearly runs into him when she opens the door to answer.

"Oh!" Beatrice says. She laughs and presses her hand over her eyes. "I didn't expect you to—"

"Would you give me a tour of the Museum?" Jordan asks her.

Beatrice looks into his eyes, trying to decode this request.

"I'm not going to give you the answers you're looking for," she says.

Jordan smiles at the ground, then looks directly at her. "But you can't blame me for trying," he says.

Beatrice looks at him, pulls the archive room door shut, and pats his chest on her way toward the reception area.

"So is that a yes?" Jordan asks, following her.

***

"We had to strip the whole building down to the studs and rebuild from scratch," Beatrice says as they finish the tour back at the reception desk. Marianne is gone, and the Museum seems completely empty.

"And of course we kept the custom woodwork intact as much as we could," Beatrice adds. "But all the walls really are brand new. They would have never taken the credit, but Tom and Jessica did like ninety percent of the work."

"Maybe that's why he never got around to renovating his own house," Jordan jokes.

Beatrice smirks and says, "That is exactly why."

Jordan can see Beatrice's expression change, a kind of dew making her eyes start to glisten.

"He would be proud what you did with it," Jordan says.

Beatrice looks around the building and smiles. "He would, wouldn't he?" she says with a nod. "I sometimes kind of think he's still here, haunting this town. Hopefully haunting this building and our lives." She sighs and shakes her head.

"I know he is," Jordan says with a laugh. "Say, can I just ask once and for all why you don't want me to compete in the treasure hunt?"

Beatrice shakes her head. "I really can't say until the treasure is found," she says. "But can *I* ask, why are you so set on finding the treasure?"

Jordan thinks about it for a second and scrubs his hand over the back of his neck. "I mean, I could say it's because it would make me feel closer to my brother," he says. "But the truth is I need to figure out what I'm doing with my life. And having some money and a place to live would help me get to the next thing."

"What is the next thing?" Beatrice asks.

"I don't know," Jordan says. "If I'm dreaming, I'd like to be a writer, to tell stories—like what I was trying to do as a journalist. But there doesn't seem to be a whole lot of lucrative opportunities for that these days, especially around here. I'll need to pivot to something else, I guess. Maybe I need to move back to the Cities. Or go back to school... Yuck."

Beatrice presses her lips together. "I didn't think I'd have many prospects in Kingsbury when I graduated," she says. "I mean, degrees in History and Theatre? But I started teaching at the school and volunteering here. I may still have a bunch of student debt, but..." She looks at the Museum around her. "You can make a life here too."

"I'd like to believe that," Jordan says. "But I'm not like you."

"What do you mean?" Beatrice asks.

Jordan sighs. "*You* know," he says. "You're..."

Brilliant, unstoppable, beautiful, Jordan thinks.

"You're Beatrice Halvorson," he says, chickening out on saying how he really feels. "The valedictorian."

Beatrice takes this in. "Maybe," she says, "it's time to start taking your own chances instead of hoping someone else will give you one. You could make a life in Kingsbury."

"How would you suggest I do that?" Jordan asks.

"I don't know," Beatrice says. "You say you want to be a writer. Start writing something. Maybe other people will like what you have to share." She touches his arm. "I would."

Jordan feels his cheeks burn, like suddenly he needs to escape from this. Escape from Beatrice.

"I need to run," Jordan says, and it comes out more abruptly than he intended.

"Okay," Beatrice says, pulling back.

Jordan smiles. "And you're still not going to let me into those archives?" he asks.

Beatrice scrunches her nose. "I'm afraid not," she says.

"Well," Jordan says, "thanks for showing me around. And tell Marianne I said goodbye."

The digital *ping* echoes through the Museum as Jordan opens the door to leave.

He looks back at the building as he walks away, and he sees Beatrice watching his retreat from the window.

Twelve

Suzy isn't one bit surprised when a gentleman with a top hat walks into Tom's Café five minutes before closing, tinkling the bell above the door.

"What now?" she mutters to Mike, who is waiting for Suzy to close shop so they can meet Paul for dinner.

"I'm looking for a Suzy Bell," the man says.

"Yeah, that's me," Suzy confirms.

"I have a horse-drawn sleigh waiting for you," the gentleman says.

"Wait," Suzy says, perking up. "Really?"

The man laughs. "Yes, really. A horse-drawn sleigh and *this*," he says, handing Suzy a golden card.

She takes in the same handwriting font from the other cards. "'It's lovely weather for a sleigh ride together'," she reads.

Now this is a present, Suzy thinks.

The man smiles and starts to make his way out of Tom's Café. "I'll wait for you outside," he says.

She looks at Mike. "Wait," she says to the man. "Can I bring a friend?"

"We have room for two," he says, tipping his hat and slipping out the door.

"Mom?" Suzy calls. "Are you okay to close up by yourself?"

Suzy's mom emerges from the kitchen with a wash bucket ready for wiping down tables. "Sure," she says. And then she sees the top hat man waiting outside the door. "What's with Ebenezer out there?" she asks.

"The latest gift," Mike says flatly.

Suzy pulls off her apron and grabs her belongings from her dad's office, then she and Mike make their way outside.

The gentleman in the top hat introduces himself as James and leads the couple to Kingsbury Municipal Golf Course. Awaiting Suzy is a literal horse-drawn sleigh.

James introduces Suzy and Mike to Spritz the Horse and Coachwoman Elizabeth. Then he helps Suzy and Mike into the sleigh, pulls a heated blanket onto their laps, and places a cup of spiced cider into each of their hands.

"This cannot be real," Suzy says as the horses start whisking the sleigh around the periphery of the golf course. "Can you believe this?" she asks Mike.

"No," he says.

Ugh, Suzy thinks, furious that one word can absolutely kill any feeling of wonder she has.

She looks at the trees and rolling, snow-covered golf course clipping by. She decides she won't let Mike's sour mood ruin this for her. She can't.

"What are you thinking about?" Suzy asks Mike.

"Nothing," he says.

And Suzy *hates* when Mike freezes her out. She's been home for all of forty-eight hours, and he's putting a damper on what very well could be a once-in-a-lifetime experience.

"It's not nothing," Suzy says. "Come on, what are you thinking about?"

Mike doesn't say anything as the sleigh continues to glide down a gradual hill. Bells affixed to the sleigh rattle as the rig navigates a slight turn.

Suzy takes a sip of her cider and waits, continuing to stare at Mike until he responds.

Then Mike finally says, "You've been acting different since Paul got into town."

"This is about *Paul?*" Suzy says.

"Is there something I should know about you two?" Mike asks.

Suzy looks at him in astonishment. "Mike," she says, forcing her hand into his. "No, there is nothing going on between me and Paul. At least romantically. Do you—I mean, have you always been concerned about me and Paul? Him and I have been friends since freshman year."

"Exactly," Mike says. "You two met when we were broken up, and when we got back together, suddenly he was always there. In every class, every story."

"We're in the same program," Suzy says. "We're in the same study group."

"You spend a *lot* of time together," Mike says. "And I'm just not there to see what that looks like. And then he's part of this series of very meaningful gifts, which I wasn't included in. And I feel like I'm not…" He pauses and then says, "I don't want to be the insecure boyfriend."

Suzy takes in everything Mike is saying and sighs. "Mike," she says, "I didn't plan this gift thing, and I have no idea who did. So whatever happens with it is more about someone else's perception of me than about what I want out of life. If I planned it, it *would* include you."

She looks at Mike, and she can tell he's trying to figure out if she's being fully honest with him.

"I mean," Suzy laughs, "you *and* this sleigh ride. Because this is pretty cool, right?"

Mike exhales. "Yes," he relents, "it is pretty cool."

"See?" Suzy says, squeezing Mike's hand and leaning her head on his shoulder.

"It's just," he says, "whoever organized this whole thing obviously knows you *very* well and didn't see me as a part of your life."

"Maybe they don't know me that well then," Suzy says.

"No," Mike says, "they do. I mean, these presents are exactly you. The golden basket this afternoon with all the terrible seasonal candies?"

"Everybody loves seasonal candies," Suzy rolls her eyes, "even if they refuse to admit it."

***

Suzy laughs so hard her Roy Rogers comes up through her nose. "Stop!" she sputters while trying to wipe her nose with a napkin.

Paul tries to stifle his own laugh. "But where did it come from?" he asks.

"It *had* to come from Spritz the Horse," Mike says. "But I have no idea how it landed in my lap!"

After the sleigh completed its third loop, Suzy and Mike made their way across town to meet Paul for dinner at Bay View Bar and Lounge.

A server comes to the table. "Are we ready to order?" she asks with a smile.

Suzy, Mike, and Paul place their orders, and Mike goes to refill the popcorn basket for the table.

Finally alone with Suzy, Paul says, "So, you're really not coming back after break?"

Suzy scrunches up her face.

"You only have a semester left," Paul says. "You're almost there."

"I don't want to be a nurse," Suzy says. "I was kidding myself being there in the first place."

"But you don't even have to be a nurse," Paul says. "Just get the degree."

"I'm not even going to take the board exam," she says.

"And that's fine," he tries to reason. "But a degree is a degree. It just shows that you're responsible, trainable, that you follow through on your commitments."

"I appreciate your concern," she says, "but it's just not going to happen. I've made my decision"

Paul shakes his head, surrendering. "Well," he says, "it won't be the same without you."

"You only have a semester left," Suzy says. "You'll be studying for your boards and applying for jobs… you won't even have time to miss me."

"Not true," Paul says. "And the whole job hunt? I've started looking, and it's bleak. Everyone says they need nurses, but then the only postings require five years' experience. It's ridiculous."

"What'd I miss?" Mike returns with the basket of popcorn—and a handful already in his mouth.

"We were just talking about spring semester," Suzy says, reasoning that it isn't a complete lie.

But then she sees Paul annoyed by her half-truth.

She takes a breath and realizes she needs to start telling people about her schooling update, and Mike is the perfect place to start.

"Actually, Mike," Suzy says, "I should tell you—"

"Suzy Bell!" a voice says from above their table.

Suzy looks up to see Laurie Banks beaming at her. She's holding a to-go box of leftovers, obviously on her way out the door.

Suzy smiles. "Laurie!" she says. "It's good to see you. You know Mike. And this is Paul, my friend from nursing school."

"Hi, Mike," Laurie says. Then she extends her hand to Paul. "It's good to meet you, Paul. I went to nursing school once a *long* time ago. I'm the clinic administrator in town now."

"Nice to meet you," Paul says.

"I was actually hoping to run into you," Laurie says conspiratorially to Suzy. "I just got notice that a nursing position is opening at the clinic this spring, and I thought of you."

"Oh," Suzy smiles, trying to keep up the charade. "Well—"

"I know you don't graduate until May," Laurie says, "but we'd love to get you plugged in. You *are* planning to come back to town, right?"

"Yes, I'm planning to move back," Suzy says.

Laurie starts digging through her purse. "Well," she says, extending a card to Suzy, "I want to see you apply. Reach out so we can chat."

Suzy looks at the card and smiles. "Great!" she says.

"Merry Christmas, all!" Laurie says, disappearing as quickly as she appeared.

Suzy sees Paul staring at her across the table, oozing disappointment.

"Whoa," Mike says, grabbing another handful of popcorn. "Did she basically just offer you a job?"

"It sure seems that way," Paul says.

Thirteen

Kara sits with her head in her hands.

"It's going to be all right," Dottie says.

"I don't even know what just happened." Kara gasps in sudden realization. "I'm going to lose my job," she says.

Dottie shakes her head. "You are not going to lose your job," she says.

Kara wipes her eyes. "You don't understand," she says. "My boss called me into his office yesterday and warned me not to get in trouble with Frank and Georgia. They have a lot of power in Kingsbury." Kara then realizes what losing her job could mean. "Am I going to have to move back in with my parents?!"

"Kara, dear," Dottie says, "you're going to need to take a deep breath."

The server at Bay View Bar and Lounge drops off a couple mugs of hot cocoa at the table.

"Thank you," Dottie says to the server. Turning back to Kara, she says, "I have known the Amundsons for a very long time, and they are not vengeful people."

"You're wrong," Kara says. "They're *awful*. I don't know what I did to deserve this. I was just trying to do something good for Tom. I was trying to help."

"I know," Dottie says. "But you have to understand there are two sides to every story. I used to read a book to my classes called *The True Story of the Three Little Pigs*. Did I ever read that to your class?"

"The one about how the Big Bad Wolf was framed?" Kara says.

"That's the one," Dottie says.

Kara shakes her head, trying to follow her second-grade teacher. "Yes," she says, "you read it to us."

Dottie nods. "Have you considered what Frank has been going through?" she asks. "Try something with me. Put yourself in his shoes."

"Like, right now?" Kara asks.

"There's no time like the present," Dottie says.

"Okay," Kara says. "I suppose he's thinking that I didn't do things exactly the way he wanted them. And that I have bad ideas. And because of that, the Festival should just be scrapped all together."

"Okay," Dottie says. "Let's take it a step further now. Why does Frank think your ideas are bad?"

Kara mulls it over.

"Take a sip of cocoa, dear," Dottie says.

Kara takes a small sip of the warm liquid chocolate, mixed with its whipped cream topping and micro marshmallows, and thinks on it some more.

Because Old Man Frank hates women, Kara thinks. And while Kara thinks that it may be true, she knows she needs to be serious about this.

"He thinks my ideas are bad because… they aren't his?" Kara says.

"Okay," Dottie says again. "Now why would his ideas be better than yours?"

Kara rolls her eyes. "Because," she says, "he thinks he knows more."

Dottie considers this, then asks, "And why does Frank think he knows more about planning the Festival?"

Kara takes a deep breath. "Because he's done it for thirty-five years," she says.

"Frank having a lot of experience would be a good reason," Dottie says. "But… your ideas and Tom's ideas have attracted more people to the Festival. Why would Frank reject ideas that bring more people to the Christmas Festival?"

"Maybe," Kara says, "bringing more people to the Festival isn't his goal."

"Hm," Dottie says. She takes a gingerly sip of her own cocoa. "You know, I was a brand-new teacher thirty-five years ago. And there was a little girl in my second-grade class. Her name was Lucy. She had these chocolate brown eyes, and she loved to sing. Oh, she would sing all day if you let her, and she had a voice as clear as a bell."

Dottie pauses, lost in the memory of this little girl.

"But come November," Dottie continues, "Lucy stopped coming to school. She was diagnosed with leukemia. It didn't look good. But she was an only child, and her parents were never going to give up. The medical bills piled up, and we loved Lucy so much. We decided that we would throw her a benefit. So just before Christmas that year, we organized something small. A silent auction, raffle prizes, platters of Christmas cookies people could purchase with a donation. And because Lucy loved to sing, we decided to do a sing-along of Lucy's favorite Christmas songs. And it would all be in Carlson Square.

"By the time the benefit rolled around, Lucy was too sick and couldn't attend. But we still held the benefit, and when it came time for the sing-along, we decided to take the party to Lucy. So the whole group of us walked over and sang all of Lucy's favorite songs right outside her house. And I can still remember Lucy being held in her dad's arms. And she sang along in that clear, strong voice of hers.

"Lucy passed away that next year. And when the holiday season rolled around again, her dad approached me and some of the other organizers of the benefit to hold a Christmas Festival to keep Lucy's memory alive. And so we did every year since."

"Frank is Lucy's dad," Kara realizes.

"Lucy Amundson is the reason the Christmas Festival exists," Dottie says. "It was always meant to be a kind of yearly celebration of her life. Sometimes time passes, and we forget the original intention of things. And I admit that I got swept away with some big, flashy ideas along the way because Lucy deserved to be celebrated in a big way. But maybe we've strayed too far."

Kara sits with this new information.

"Why haven't I heard this story before?" Kara asks.

"I think it's too painful for Frank or Georgia to share," Dottie shrugs. "And everybody else—myself included—feels like it's not our story to share. So... I guess it ends up not being told at all."

Kara replays her arguments with Frank in her head and can hardly stand to think how she came off.

"Ugh," Kara says. "Now I feel absolutely rotten."

"You didn't know," Dottie says. "And although I can't say for sure, I don't think Tom knew either."

"There's no way he did," Kara says.

Why don't people communicate?! she thinks.

"Is there a way I could make things right with Frank?" Kara asks.

Dottie smiles. "Maybe just talking to him about it would help," she says. "But I'm really not sure."

They both take a sip of their cocoa.

"It's just a shame there won't be a Festival at all this year," Kara says. "Maybe we could have done something to get it back on track. And maybe it would have been the perfect way to honor *both* Lucy and Tom."

"Now who says we can't still have something?" Dottie asks.

"Uh," Kara says, "the mayor, the City Council, Frank. Insurance, permits… You were there."

"Yes, I was," Dottie says. "And I heard them say you could still hold an event at a private venue."

"I don't have a private venue," Kara says.

Dottie shakes her head. "Your parents own a coffee shop. Wouldn't Tom's Café be the perfect place to host an event in his and Lucy's honor?"

"Oh," Kara shakes her head, "I really don't want to drag my family into this."

"I don't see why not," Dottie says. "But I suppose there are other businesses we could ask. What about that cute little place that just opened—the Roundhouse?"

"The Wheelhouse," Kara corrects her.

"Doesn't your boyfriend own the place?" Dottie asks.

"Boyfriend?" Kara says.

"It's a small town, dear," Dottie says. "Word gets around when you go on a date in broad daylight."

"It was coffee," Kara says.

"I heard it got a little heated," Dottie smiles.

Kara is taken aback. "That," she says, "was because of the argument with—"

"I'm just trying to ruffle your feathers," Dottie says. "The point is that you could ask him to host."

Kara thinks for a moment. "Since he just opened, I suppose it could be a good advertising opportunity for him," she says, "to get him connected to the community."

"See?" Dottie says.

"Well," Kara shrugs, "it doesn't hurt to ask."

THURSDAY, DECEMBER 22

Fourteen

Jordan approaches Carlson Square just as five o'clock strikes, and gentle piano music starts mounting from the speakers.

The Square is filled with people, many of which aren't even searching for the treasure. The mini performances that are part of the clue reveals have taken on an attraction of their own, drawing crowds night after night—each turnout larger than the last.

After the children's choir on Monday and the Sugar Plum Fairy on Tuesday, Wednesday's reveal included a live twenty-piece orchestra playing "The Twelve Days of Christmas" and a cast of seventy-eight actors doing a slap comedy routine as the items in the list. The performance culminated in a banner being unraveled with the third clue:

I once thought I was frightened
By the simple act of flying;
But in truth, I was frightened
By falling to the ground.
Now I don't fear falling,
And I dream now of flying;
I finally see birds winging
Ever since you came around.

Jordan has no idea what this clue means—or its connection to anything in Kingsbury. Cross-analyzing it with the first two clues just makes his head spin. So between his cluelessness and Beatrice's discouragement, he decided to focus yesterday and today on his article about *The Kingsbury Gazette*, completing his first draft.

So at least there's that, Jordan thinks to himself.

The piano music continues as curtains obscuring a portion of the Square part and reveal a woman dressed in a flowing white gown, her skin dusted with gold and her head sprouting an ornate gold crown spreading itself in all directions.

She opens her mouth, and the entire crowd is transfixed as her soprano voice soars with the words of "Ave Maria".

About a minute into the performance, Jordan almost jumps out of his skin when a camel—a real life *camel*—walks past him toward the stage. He looks around to find other animals and their handlers coming from other directions toward the stage—a donkey, a few goats, a whole herd of sheep.

This must have cost a fortune, Jordan thinks. *Where did Tom get this kind of money?!*

And as the song builds, the woman in white starts to ascend into the sky. She has to be standing on some kind of scissor lift, but Jordan doesn't see anything beneath her. Her dress drapes at impossible lengths to follow her up into the air, then is pulled away to reveal a live Nativity scene—Mary, Joseph, Baby Jesus, shepherds, and wisemen all accounted for.

As the angel softly sings the final strains of "Ave Maria", the entire crowd is silent and still. Jordan looks over, and a woman nearby has tear stains running down her cheeks.

The piano sounds its last notes, and the crowd erupts in applause. Then, as happened the previous nights, the next clue is revealed:

It's curious to watch
Something fall apart.
It's partially science;
It's partially art.
Science is clear:
It's rust and erosion.
Art is more subtle:
It's sense and emotion.
Is observing what was
Become something new
Make that thing the lesser
For what it went through?
Or is something more valuable
To evolve and keep living?
It's science to change;
It's art to keep giving.

Jordan is mystified by what any of this means. He wonders if it's even good poetry.

At least the performance was amazing, he thinks.

"Hey," Beatrice says from beside him.

"Hey," Jordan says back, still embarrassed how he left her at the Museum yesterday.

"I didn't see you at yesterday's clue reveal," she says.

"I was here," he says. "I was just consumed with my *Gazette* article and couldn't stick around. But I've been wanting to tell you that what you're doing here is amazing."

"Oh," Beatrice says, "thank you."

"It's really impressive," he says. "How did you do the angel lifting off the ground thing?"

"Theatre magic," Beatrice says with a straight face.

Jordan smiles. "Of course," he says.

Beatrice laughs and touches Jordan's arm. "I'm just glad tomorrow is the last night," she says.

"I bet," Jordan says. "What does Tom have in store for us?"

Beatrice shakes her head. "You'll have to wait and see," she says.

"*There's* that mysterious thing you have going," Jordan says.

"Ugh," Beatrice says. "Please know that it brings me no pleasure. After this is all over, I'd love to spill everything."

"Over dinner?" Jordan says.

Beatrice searches Jordan's face.

For a moment, Jordan panics. *This is a threshold I can't uncross*, he thinks.

But then he decides to double down.

"Will you go on a date with me?" he asks.

Beatrice cocks her head and grins. "I thought you would never ask," she says.

"Is that a yes?" Jordan says.

"Yes," she says, "But fair warning, me spilling everything over dinner will include a lot of complaining about your brother and how self-involved he can be, even from the grave."

Jordan laughs. "I can definitely be a sounding board for that," he says.

"He's lucky that I love a grand gesture as much as the next person," Beatrice rolls her eyes.

Grand gesture? Jordan thinks.

"Also," he says, "I want to apologize."

"For what?" Beatrice says, confused.

"I've been pushing you to reveal things about the treasure hunt that you obviously can't share," Jordan says. "I shouldn't have put you in that position. So I just need to say I'm sorry."

Beatrice takes a deep breath. "I appreciate that, but I never felt compelled to spill any information to you," she says. "You're not exactly good at coaxing information from people."

Jordan shrugs. "Very fair," he concedes.

"But," Beatrice says, "if you feel bad and want to make it up to me, I have a request."

"Shoot," Jordan says.

Beatrice scrunches up her nose. "Could I see Tom's house?" she asks. "And just to be clear, this is not like the executor of Tom's estate coming in to make sure you didn't ruin it. I'm just curious what you've done with the place."

"Of course," says Jordan. "When?"

"Lunch tomorrow?" Beatrice asks.

***

Jordan can't help but reflect on Beatrice's words from the past few days on his way home.

This treasure hunt isn't meant for you.

I wonder if he intended such a large audience.

He's lucky that I love a grand gesture as much as the next person.

Jordan thinks about grand gestures and intentions and, yes, love.

Maybe it's because he has all these things on his own brain.

But it comes to him in a flash.

He knows exactly who Tom's last grand gesture was meant for.

Fifteen

Suzy is already preparing for shop-close when the bell above the door tinkles.

"Did I make it in time?" Marianne Joki asks.

Suzy checks the time as five o'clock strikes.

"You're cutting it pretty close," Suzy says, "but yes. What can I get you?"

"Well, I had one of your eggnog scones earlier," Marianne says. "And I just couldn't stop thinking about it. I was hoping to buy more if you have any left."

Suzy smiles, loving to hear how one of her creations can stay with people long after it's been devoured.

"I'm glad to hear you like them," Suzy says, glancing at the display case. "We have three left. How many can I box up for you?"

"I have to take all three," Marianne says. "They're simply too good."

As they complete their transaction and Suzy boxes up the scones, the bell above the door tinkles again.

"Oh, good. You're still open," Georgia Amundson says as she walks into the shop with her husband Frank in tow.

And Suzy's jaw nearly drops to the floor.

Suzy heard all about the scuffle between her sister and Frank at the City Council meeting yesterday. And now Frank and Georgia casually waltz into her family's shop?

The gall of these people, she thinks.

And yet, Suzy admits the Amundsons' ability to dissociate is an absolute endorsement for the idea that you can't live in a small town without doing a lot of forgiving, forgetting, and moving on.

"You need some last-minute goodies too?" Marianne asks the couple.

"We're going over to the Dillans' house for dinner," Georgia says. "But Frank's back was hurting him, so we weren't sure. But now we are." Georgia shakes her head and sighs. "This is my dessert contribution in a pinch."

"We are so lucky when Suzy's in town," Marianne says, giving Suzy a wink. "Have a good night, all."

Suzy smiles as Marianne waves and makes her exit.

"So, what can I get you?" Suzy asks Georgia.

Georgia steps up to the dessert display case. "Well," she says, "what do you have left?"

Suzy takes a look, and the case looks sparse—a great sign that she estimated Kingsbury's appetite for desserts correctly today.

"There's a few giant ginger cookies, a couple Mini Monkey Bread muffins, and one figgy bread pudding," Suzy says.

Georgia hems and haws as Frank picks up a copy of the newest *Gazette* from the counter. "Christmas Festival Canceled" is the front-page headline, and Suzy looks to see his reaction—good, bad, or otherwise. He doesn't seem to react, but Suzy thinks he looks a little pale.

Georgia laughs. "We're going to have to get them all," she says.

"Sounds good to me," Suzy smiles.

Georgia hands over cash, and Suzy goes to box up the order.

"Actually," Georgia says, "would you mind heating them up? Would that make them fresher?"

"They were made this morning," Suzy says, "so they're fresh. But I'm happy to give them a little warmth. That way, they'll smell really good when you hand them over to Marcie Dillan."

"Ha!" Georgia says. "You are a mind reader. Yes, please warm them up."

Georgia and Frank take a seat in the dining area as Suzy places the cookies, muffins, and bread pudding on a tray for their countertop warming oven.

As Suzy loads them in the warmer and sets the timer, a yawn escapes her mouth. It was a busy day at the shop, thanks in part to another golden birthday present—this time, a string quartet that played two hours of Suzy's favorite pop songs throughout the morning. Word got around town about the surprise performance, and it ended up attracting a full house of customers.

And truthfully, Suzy was impressed by how she handled the influx of people, considering her lack of sleep last night. She just couldn't stop thinking about the way Paul was so disappointed in her—and how disappointed she was in herself—that she couldn't muster up the courage to tell Mike or her parents or anyone about quitting school.

Add onto that the mystery of the gift giver and a newfound feeling of guilt at blindly accepting some of the more lavished gifts (a golden envelope from last night simply included one thousand dollars cash), and Suzy eventually gave up on sleep and headed to the Café.

She spent the early hours of the morning organizing the bar area and then deep cleaning the dining area and both bathrooms. By four o'clock, she found nothing left to vacuum, dust, or sanitize. And when her mom walked in the door at five o'clock, all her desserts for the day were either baking or ready to bake, and Suzy was testing out a new creation, the Christmas Tree Farm Latte.

Suzy's mom walks out from the office and is surprised when she sees Frank and Georgia in the shop. She makes eye contact with Suzy, who just shrugs.

"I forgot to tell you," Suzy's mom says, "Laurie Banks came in while you were in back this morning. She said she talked to you about a nursing job for when you graduate?"

"Oh," Suzy says, keeping her eyes on the small warming oven. "Yeah, she did. But I haven't had much time to think about it."

"What's to think about?" her mom says. "It'd be a good place to get your feet wet. And if you want, you can stay at home until your student loans are paid off. I know it's probably not what you'd want. But with a nurse's salary, you could be debt-free in no time and then be set up to go anywhere you want—even though I'd love if you stayed nearby."

Even with her lack of sleep last night, Suzy didn't feel all that tired until right now.

Maybe it's time to put this whole charade to rest, she thinks. *So I dropped out of school... So I don't want to be a nurse... So what? Shouldn't I just be honest? Isn't telling difficult truths what being an adult is all about?*

But then again, she thinks, *isn't the reality that I accumulated a mountain of debt going to nursing school something I also have to face—and pay for? Isn't being responsible for your actions also what being an adult is all about?*

Or Plan C, Suzy thinks. *Maybe I should leave the shop right now, find Tom's treasure, and lay claim to his estate…*

If only Suzy could make heads or tails of any of those impossible treasure hunt clues…

"I'd actually like to be closer to home too," Suzy says to her mom. "I'm just not sure if that's the job for me."

Her mom leans against the counter and nods. "I can understand that," she says. "From what I hear, being a clinic nurse isn't for everyone. I mean, I see you hustle and bustle around here. You like the action."

"Exactly," Suzy says.

"You like working alongside and with people," her mom adds.

"Right," Suzy agrees.

"And maybe working in a hospital setting might be better," her mom concludes, "especially while you're just starting out."

NO, Suzy thinks.

"I mean, I could never do it," her mom says. "But you're so good in a crisis. You'd be great in the emergency room. You'd be fantastic anywhere, really."

Suzy removes the cookies, muffins, and bread pudding—warmed to perfection—and boxes them up for Georgia and Frank.

"Well," Suzy says, "I… guess I just look at what's available at the hospital and apply." She tries to smile at her mom, but she's afraid it comes off as disingenuous.

Her mom reaches out and rubs Suzy's arm, and Suzy wonders if her mom sees right through the façade. Deep down, Suzy knows she does.

But this isn't the time or place to talk about it, Suzy thinks.

And maybe that's the problem. It's never the time or place to talk about the deepest burdens—at least not until they've already become the darkest and most destructive versions of themselves.

Suzy is disappointed in herself. How did the thing she *should* do unravel from the thing she *could* do to become the thing she *would* do? And why was dropping out of nursing school so easy and liberating, but telling people about that decision so difficult and shameful?

Suzy brings the box to the counter. "There you be," she says to Georgia and Frank.

Georgia stands and picks up the box, taking a deep whiff. "They smell delicious," she says. "Thank you."

"Of course," Suzy says. "Can I get you anything else?" She looks at Georgia, who is beaming, then to Frank, who looks strangely out of breath after standing up from his own chair.

"I think we're set," Georgia says.

But Suzy feels that something is wrong. Frank's coloring, the way he holds his shoulders. Something deeper is happening.

"Frank," Suzy asks, "are you feeling all right?"

"He'll be fine," Georgia says. "Frank, are you ready?"

And then Frank falls.

He knocks over a chair on his way to the ground and sprawls across the floor of Tom's Café.

Suzy's mom and Georgia are instantly on the ground by his side, trying to get him to sit upright or respond at all.

"Frank?!" Georgia shrieks.

And now Suzy's mom is asking for Suzy to help—administer CPR, or something… anything.

And Suzy feels like she's watching a movie, a spectator more than a participant. Frozen where she stands, accumulating dust and humiliation.

Suzy's mom runs past her to call for an ambulance.

Ear pressed to the phone, her mom grabs Suzy's arm. "Is there anything you can do to help?" she asks.

No, Suzy thinks. *No, there's not.*

Sixteen

Kara takes a deep breath and enters The Wheelhouse.

"Hi," Kara says to the server at the reception counter. "I'm looking for Brent."

"Sure," he says. "I'll go grab him."

When Brent comes out from the kitchen and sees Kara standing there, she smiles.

"Uh oh," he says.

"Uh oh?" she asks. "What kind of greeting is that?"

Brent laughs at her. "The last time I saw you, you were trying to drop kick a snowbank," he says. "And the time before that, you got into a public argument in my dining room."

"I can see how that makes me look," Kara says. "But I have a proposition for you."

"I'm intrigued," he says. "What's up?"

"Well," Kara starts, "did you hear that the Christmas Festival may not be happening tomorrow?"

"Yes, one of my team members told me," Brent nods.

"The reason it's not happening is because there's no place to host it," Kara says. "I'm wondering if we could possibly clear the snow off your patio and use The Wheelhouse as a gathering space."

Kara can almost see the wheels turning in Brent's head.

"There's going to be a lot less people than a normal year," she says. "Maybe less Festival, more... Picnic."

"A Christmas Picnic?" Brent asks. "In the evening?"

"Whatever," Kara says. "We'll still call it the Christmas Festival. The point is… we would invite people, there would be a few vendor booths to give something for people to do, and you could advertise for your amazing new restaurant by giving back to the community with free cider or little appetizers."

"Oh," Brent says, "so now I'm hosting a community festival and giving away free food and beverage?"

"…Yes?" Kara says with a smile.

Brent looks at her for a moment, and Kara shrugs to emphasize her question in the air.

"It's a good thing I like you," Brent says.

***

"How do you feel about string lights?" Brent asks.

After they cleared snow from The Wheelhouse's patio and then decided to expand the party area into the side lot next to the restaurant, Kara and Brent started mapping out where everything—vendor tents, outdoor warmers, seating, a cluster of campfire stoves for marshmallow roasting, Santa's sleigh—could be set up throughout the space.

"It's like you read my mind," Kara says.

"Don't get too excited," Brent returns. "They're string lights I have set aside for the patio during the *summer*, not Christmas colors or anything."

"They sound perfect," Kara says.

Brent is back quickly, and the two start unboxing the lights.

"So I have a question," Brent says.

"Sure," Kara says, opening each box of lights in succession.

"I can understand a business holding an event," he says. "With the advertising and community building, there's something to gain—new customers, more revenue. But what possesses people to hold just a general community event? I don't get it."

"That's a good question," Kara says, genuinely at a loss. "I… don't know."

"Well," Brent says, "you're organizing this whole thing. What got you interested?"

And she knows the answer to that question. "My brother used to do it," she says, "so this is my way of honoring him."

"I guess inheriting a tradition makes sense," Brent says. "Do you know why he got involved?"

Kara thinks about it and draws a blank. "I'm actually not sure," she says. "But a restaurant is like a community event, right?"

"I'm not sure what you're getting at," Brent says.

"Me neither," Kara says, "but let's just play it out."

"Okay, sure," Brent says. "Proceed."

"A restaurant is like a community event," she repeats. "You offer up a space to gather, people get together, you serve them food and drinks. And you do it almost every day of the year. So…" Kara thinks, "making money aside, what possesses *you* to run a restaurant?"

Brent thinks about it. "You're clever," he says.

"Well?" she asks with a smile. "I'm waiting for an answer. There are easier ways to make money. So out of all the business possibilities, what possesses you to run a restaurant?"

"Huh, let's think," Brent says, putting down a tangle of string lights. "I guess when I drill down on it, I run a restaurant because one of the best parts of life is people connecting with each other. And I want to spend my time creating a place where the best parts of life can happen."

Kara smiles.

"What?" Brent asks, smiling in return.

"Nothing," Kara says. "It's just, that's kind of beautiful." She shrugs.

"What can I say?" Brent says. "You've got me waxing philosophical."

"So now let's close the loop," Kara says. "Connecting with each other is the best part of life. And somebody might live in a community where there's a gap in the market of connecting with others."

"Gap in the market?" Brent teases her. "You're speaking my language!"

Kara laughs. "So," she continues, "some people plan a one-day festival. And others…" she motions to Brent.

"Open a restaurant," Brent says.

"Exactly. So *that's* what possesses people to hold a general community event. To contribute to people connecting," says Kara, taking a deep breath of cold air. "And I suppose that's why they *keep* holding events too, even when it's nearly impossible."

"I think what you're doing with saving the Christmas Festival is really great," Brent says.

"Or absolutely insane," Kara suggests.

"There's just one thing I don't get," Brent says.

"Yeah?" Kara asks.

"You could have gone to any business in town to help save the Festival," he says.

"Not *any* business," Kara says.

"Why did you come to me?" Brent asks.

Kara looks down as she untangles a bundle of lights.

"Maybe I know a good guy when I see one," she says, looking at him.

Brent grins at her.

"Or maybe I just think you're cute," she shrugs.

Brent looks behind him and then snaps back to Kara, pointing at himself. "You think I'm cute?" he asks.

"I said what I said," Kara says. "Now, there's just one thing *I* don't get."

"Yeah?" Brent asks.

"When Wendy came into your restaurant and said she wanted to set you up with her friend," Kara says, "why did you agree to meet with me?"

"Because one of the best parts of life is people connecting with each other," he says, echoing his words from before. "And... I had already noticed you around town."

"Noticed me?" Kara asks. "That's kind of creepy."

"Well?" Brent says. "You're hot."

"Shut up," Kara says with a laugh. "And how do you feel after seeing me have an argument across your restaurant and attack a snowbank?"

"The first impression stands," Brent says. "Hot."

Kara tries to push down her smile.

"Okay," Kara says. "We need to get these lights up."

Brent smiles at her and says, "Whatever you say, boss."

FRIDAY, DECEMBER 23

Seventeen

Jordan balances two mugs of tea and a bottle of honey as he walks into Tom's small living room.

"So how does it feel to be back in town?" he asks Jessica.

"It's kind of strange," Jessica says from the couch. "Kind of nice. Kind of sad. Kind of overdue."

When Jordan reached out to Jessica last night, it seems they were on the same wavelength about her paying a visit back to Kingsbury for the Christmas Festival. She said she saw a news story about the treasure hunt for Tom's estate and felt like she needed to return and get some closure—and also visit her parents.

"I know what you mean," Jordan says, setting down the mugs and the honey on a coffee table, then settling into a chair opposite the couch.

"Thanks," Jessica says, pulling a mug close to her and pulling at the bag of tea.

"It seems like Tom is everywhere I look," Jordan says.

"You *do* live in his house," Jessica says with a laugh, looking around. "Even though you've basically stripped him away from this interior. The place is basically brand new."

"Cosmetic fixes," Jordan bats away her compliment. "And I haven't done anything to the exterior."

"Rehanging drywall is *not* a cosmetic fix," Jessica says. "And I'm sure you'll keep going on the outside once spring rolls around anyway."

Jordan shakes his head. "Probably not," he says. "The house is part of Tom's estate, and whoever wins the treasure hunt gets the house."

"Really?" Jessica asks. "The prize would include the house too?"

"The prize is his entire estate," Jordan says.

"I guess I'm confused," she says. "Why would you put *any* money into this dump then?" She shakes her head. "Sorry, that was very forward."

"It's okay," Jordan says. "I ask myself the same thing." He jerks the tea bag around in his cup and pulls it out, stirring and adding honey. "I suppose it's my version of therapy. My *expensive* version of therapy."

"Ha!" Jessica says. "Have you been to therapy lately? Because I have, and I think a mini house reno may be the *inexpensive* version."

"If you say so," Jordan says, risking burning his mouth for a sip of tea.

"Tom loved when he bought this place," Jessica says. "The whole history of it as one of the railroad worker housing bungalows when there was a housing shortage during World War I... He was so excited when one finally went on the market for so cheap. *And* he'd be impressed with you fixing it up like you did."

"Actually," Jordan says, "he would have criticized my lack of finesse with said drywall."

"Beneath all that," Jessica says, "he would have been proud. I'm not sure why siblings have such a hard time complimenting each other." She shakes her head as she prepares her own tea. "Clearly I'm an only child."

Jordan smiles at a memory. "There was one time," Jordan says, "when Tom was in fourth grade and I was in first. I had drawn a freehand picture of a Pokémon, and Tom was so impressed with it. The next day he brought it on the school bus with us and showed all his friends and was bragging about how amazing his little brother was."

Jessica smiles. "I love that," she says.

"We didn't always see eye-to-eye," Jordan says. "But… I miss him."

"Me too," Jessica says. "I'm just grateful we had him for the time we did." She wipes a tear from her eye. "Uh, I knew I would cry today."

A knock sounds at the door, and Jordan goes to answer it.

"I'm early," Beatrice says from behind a paper grocery bag in her arms.

"Not at all," Jordan says. "Jessica and I were just—"

"Jessica?" Beatrice says, surprised to see Tom's girlfriend on the couch with a cup of tea.

"Beatrice," Jessica pouts and runs over to give her friend a good, long hug.

"I'm so happy to see you," Beatrice says, wiping her own eyes and laughing. "I didn't know you were in town."

"This was my first stop," Jessica says. "I was just telling Jordan that I felt like the Christmas Festival was the perfect occasion for me to come back and get some closure."

"It's going to be different this year," Beatrice says. "There were a few bumps with the planning this past week, but there's still going to be something. Promise me that you're going to be in Carlson Square at five tonight."

"Done," Jessica says. "And we'll need to find time to get together properly before I leave on the twenty-sixth."

"Done," Beatrice smiles.

"I should really get over to my parents' house," Jessica says. "We're going out for lunch at some new place in the old Rainbow Ice Cream building?"

"The Wheelhouse," Beatrice says.

"Is it any good?" Jessica asks.

"Surprisingly, yes," Beatrice says. "And that's where some of the stuff for the Christmas Festival will be tonight, so you'll get a little preview."

"Before you go," Jordan says to Jessica. "I'm curious if you've heard anything more about the treasure hunt."

"No," Jessica says. "Only what I saw on TV."

"You should take a look at the clues," Beatrice jumps in. "I mean, Tom organized the whole thing, so…"

I knew it, Jordan thinks.

Jordan grabs a paper with a copy of the clues written down from the kitchen. "Yeah, take a look," he says. "Tell us what you think."

Jessica reads through the four clues, and she starts laughing.

"What is it?" Jordan asks.

"These aren't clues," Jessica says. "They're Tom's stupid little poems."

"What do you mean?" Jordan asks.

"Sorry," Jessica clarifies, "they're not stupid. They're just… when Tom was trying to figure something out, he would put his thoughts into verse. He had some theory that rhyming unlocked some kind of higher dimension in your brain or something. He called them his 'musings'. He had hundreds of them. I still have a notebook somewhere."

"Funny," Jordan says. "Why would he pass them off as clues for a treasure hunt in Kingsbury, do you think?"

"No idea," Jessica shrugs, "but there's only one place where Tom would hide a treasure in this town. That man was a creature of habit if I ever saw one."

Jordan looks at Beatrice, and she's grinning like a devil.

"Where?" Jordan asks.

"There's this little hidey-hole in the foot bridge over Kingsbury Creek by the baseball field," Jessica says. "When we were in high school, Tom used to leave surprises for me in there. I haven't even been back there for… ten years, maybe?"

"Well, are you going to go check it now?" Beatrice asks. "You could win Tom's estate."

Jessica considers it for a moment.

Jordan and Beatrice exchange knowing glances.

"No," she says.

"What?" Jordan asks.

"Why?" Beatrice follows.

"I came here to get closure, not to open up the wound again," Jessica says. "I think I need to be grateful for the time I had here with Tom and move on."

Jessica grabs her belongings, thanks Jordan for the tea, and says she'll see both him and Beatrice at the Festival.

As the door closes and Jessica walks away from the house, Jordan and Beatrice stand there in silence.

"Who in their right mind," Beatrice says, "passes up a quarter-million-dollar estate?"

Jordan shrugs. "I guess Jessica," he says.

Beatrice starts back toward the door.

"Where are you going?" Jordan asks.

"I've been planning this treasure hunt for a year," Beatrice says. "I'm gonna see what Tom hid. Are you coming?"

"You didn't know where the treasure led?" Jordan asks. "*Or* what the token is?"

"Are you kidding?" Beatrice says. "Tom didn't trust me with any of his secrets."

Jordan pulls on his boots. "And you organized the whole thing anyway?"

"It was my childhood best friend's post-mortem directive," Beatrice says. "I didn't really have a choice."

***

Jordan and Beatrice venture to the foot bridge and, with no one in sight, inspect the entire thing until Jordan finds a hidden shelf just underneath the bridge span.

He reaches in and comes back with a small box sealed in a plastic bag.

Jordan opens the plastic bag and drops the small box into his bare hand.

"Open it," Beatrice whispers.

Eighteen

Suzy doesn't look to see who enters her bedroom. She doesn't unroll from her blanket. She doesn't open the drapes or turn on the light. She doesn't care.

"Hey, birthday girl," her dad says, sitting on the foot of her bed. "I found another gift for you. It was on top of the garbage bin outside."

Suzy feels another wave of grief coming over her, and it's like her chest caves in on itself. She tries to tell herself she's being too hard on herself, that figuring out what you want to do with your life is difficult for everyone. *Even people who know exactly what path their life will take get discouraged,* she tells herself.

And then she sees Frank lying on the floor of the shop, lifeless as his wife wails and her mom rushes past her to call an ambulance.

Suzy eventually peeks out of her blanket cocoon and sees her dad still sitting there, the latest golden gift in his hands.

"You can put it with the others," she mutters.

Her dad stands up and places the gift alongside six other untouched gifts on her dresser.

Suzy thinks her dad will drop the present and leave her to rot in bed, but he takes a seat back on the bed.

"Do you want to talk about it?" he asks.

"No," Suzy says.

She can hear her dad take a deep breath, and she rolls her eyes.

Take a hint, she thinks. *I don't want to talk.*

"Last year," Suzy's dad says, "I was talking to Tom. He was having a rough day, and he said he wanted to quit his paramedic job and become a plumber."

This information is so absurd that Suzy can't stay quiet. "A plumber?" Suzy says.

"He said he liked helping people but that he couldn't see himself working out of an ambulance—or in the medical field at all—for the next thirty years," her dad says. "He was planning to quit his job the next day. And do you know what I said?"

"That he was crazy?" Suzy asks.

"I told him that he had a good, steady job," Suzy's dad says. "I said that he shouldn't throw that away just because he had a bad day. And when he said that he'd been feeling that way for a few years, I told him that work can be tough to endure sometimes but that we do it to make money, not to have fun."

Suzy's dad clears his throat.

"He said that plumbing is a lucrative business, that he could own his own company, that he'd be able to help people in need and feel like he accomplished something with every project he finished," he says. "And I told him that you don't own a business, that a business owns you."

It's kind of true, Suzy thinks, considering the lack of vacation time her parents have had over the years.

"And so, he continued working as a paramedic," Suzy's dad says. "And the next week, that car ran through the crash scene and killed him."

In some ways, Suzy remembers everything that happened since then—the disbelief, the heartache, the tears. She remembers hearing her dad sobbing in the middle of the night and her mom hugging her for twenty minutes straight.

In other ways, Suzy doesn't feel like it happened at all—that Tom will come bounding through her bedroom door and look through her things just to annoy her.

But what she remembers for certain is how she felt full and sure and confident one day, then felt empty and hesitant and uncertain the next. And she spent the last year questioning where she belonged, what she was going to do with her life, how she would continue to breathe and move and be.

And she remembers how the ground eventually gave way to the realization that every moment holds a choice. And that choice is hers alone. And that realization is a perpetual golden gift of perspective and autonomy amidst a dark plague of hopelessness and tyranny.

Suzy unwraps herself from her blanket. "Tom didn't die because you told him to keep working," she says.

Her dad grins and shakes Suzy's leg. "I know," he says. "But the part of me that thinks I had a role in it says that I need to dole out better advice to my children."

It's time, Suzy thinks.

She sits up next to her dad. "I dropped out of nursing school," she says.

The words hang there in the air, finally.

"Oh, Suzy," he says, squeezing her foot. "What happened?"

"I don't know," she says. "When Tom died, I took a hard look at what I wanted out of life. And I realized that I was going into nursing for the wrong reasons. It's a good, important job. It's just... not the job for me."

Her dad takes a deep breath.

"I think you did the right thing then," he says. "So now what are you going to do? You still have to find a way to make money."

"I know," Suzy says. "I've thought long and hard about it, and... I want to take over the Café. I want to learn the ropes from you and mom and, when you're ready to retire, take it over completely."

Suzy's dad sighs. "Your mom and I worked our tails off to keep that place open throughout the years," he says. "It's not easy to be in business."

"I know," Suzy says. "But I'm not afraid. And this is what I've dreamed of my entire life. I have ideas on how to expand the dessert portion of the business. *This* is what I'm meant to do. This is what's inside of me. This is what I need to bring to the world."

"Well," her dad says, "then I'm happy to help show you the ropes. And I've worried about what would happen to the business when I wanted to retire, so maybe I'm a bit relieved to know it will live on."

"I..." Suzy pauses. "I don't know how to tell mom that I quit school," she says.

"She was proud of you going to school for nursing," Suzy's dad says. "And you're right. She might be a little disappointed."

"Great," Suzy says with sarcasm.

"But," he continues, "she wants to see you do amazing things with your life, and she can't make your decisions for you."

"I just don't know how to tell her," Suzy says. "I don't know how to tell anyone. Mike doesn't even know."

"Then don't," Suzy's dad shrugs.

"What?" Suzy asks.

He says, "Don't tell them."

"I've tried that," Suzy says. "I need to say something."

"No," he says, "I mean, don't just tell them. *Show* them. You want to expand dessert options at the Café? Use the Christmas Festival tonight to launch."

"Really?" Suzy asks.

"Absolutely," her dad says. "I was talking to Kara, and the Festival tonight is going to be scaled back and based at The Wheelhouse. If there are changes, it seems like a perfect year to switch things up. So what are you going to make that the crowds are going to flock to our booth for?"

Suzy smiles, exhilarated by the sudden freedom she feels. "It's a Festival," she says, "so it needs to be easy to eat."

"Agreed," Suzy's dad says. "It should either be in a cup, in a cone, or on a stick."

"And it's cold out," Suzy says, "so it should be something that won't require too much handling without gloves. And it should be warm."

"I like where you're headed," her dad smiles.

"And it's Christmas, so it should be nostalgic," Suzy adds. "Something that's familiar and simple, but something they can't make or get easily themselves."

"Okay," her dad nods. "And?"

Suzy thinks. "And it has to be inexpensive and fast to make, so we can maximize revenue."

Suzy's dad laughs. "You're a natural," he says. "So what is it going to be?"

Suzy runs down the list in her head again, and her mind combines layers of ideas until she's found a keeper.

"Deep fried Christmas cookies," she says.

"What?" Suzy's dad asks.

"I make three different types of dough from popular Christmas cookies. Maybe sugar cookies, gingerbread, and... peanut butter blossoms?" she says. "I would stack them on a stick and deep fry them. Maybe sprinkle them with powdered sugar or drizzle them with some kind of glaze or frosting."

Her dad smiles. "How do you know how to do all this?" he asks.

"What do you mean?" Suzy asks.

"Coming up with recipes like that," he says. "I've never heard of... deep friend Christmas cookies."

Suzy shrugs. "I don't know," she says. "I like desserts. And food is more about mixing and matching components than about a set menu of recipes, so I play around with them. Not all of them work out."

"Does that mean you'll have to make a test batch of these cookie things you just dreamed up?" her dad asks.

"That would definitely have to happen," she says. "Do we have any oil for deep frying?"

"If we don't, I'll go straight to the store to get some," he says, taking off out of her room.

"Dad," she calls after him, "I need to make sure we have all the other ingredients too!"

Nineteen

Kara takes a breath as five o'clock finally arrives, and she suddenly feels a sense of relief that she has done everything she can for the Christmas Festival. Whether it goes well or not is now out of her hands.

What will happen, she thinks, *will happen.*

This thought strikes her unexpectedly as she watches the people across the street in Carlson Square settle down as a twenty-piece orchestra stops tuning their instruments for a few moments as a conductor takes the stand and then gives a cue.

Kara walks over to see the clue reveal spectacle in its last night, and the number of performers seems to rival the number of people assembled. Besides the orchestra, there's a children's choir behind the instruments, a troupe of ballerinas bowing low to the ground in front of the orchestra, a whole host of people dressed in "The Twelve Days of Christmas" costumes to one side behind the choir, and what looks like a live Nativity scene to the other.

The assemblage of people makes Kara think she should have made more of a point to attend the performances on the previous nights.

As the music begins, the children's choir sings a few bars. And then a man in a tuxedo steps forward and starts singing opera in Italian. She doesn't recognize the song until the orchestra swells in earnest for the first time, and she realizes it's "Nessun Dorma", which she really only knows from a random liberal arts elective she took in college.

Across the Square, Kara sees a woman wearing a white gown and holding a glowing white paper lantern with both hands. And it's not long before Kara realizes women in dresses—wedding dresses?—and paper lanterns filtering into Carlson Square from every direction.

The women circulate through the crowd as a woman opera singer and the children's choir sing a couple lines. Then the man in the tuxedo takes over for a deep swell of music. And when the song reaches its climax, the women in the wedding dresses release their paper lanterns. A hundred-some lanterns float into the sky as everyone in the Square gawks upward and erupts into applause.

Kara can hardly believe what just happened as the song ends and a large banner at the front of the park unravels next to four others already unraveled from previous nights.

> Who are we in the end
> When the sands of time have fallen?
> What difference did we really make
> When the loans are all called in?
> We cannot choose how we're remembered,
> But we're wise to keep in mind
> Our legacy is composed and sealed
> By the ones we leave behind.

Kara's eyes wash over her late brother's words as she makes her way back to The Wheelhouse.

Our legacy is composed and sealed by the ones we leave behind, she repeats to herself.

Christmas in Kingsbury 131

As she sees the people migrate from the Square to the vendor tents set up at The Wheelhouse, she watches the campfires send ash into the cold sky and servers distributing free cider and stacks of piping hot grilled cheese sandwiches. Kara wonders if this is the legacy Tom hoped to leave behind. If this is enough.

Would it ever be enough? she thinks.

Part of her knows that even one person honoring your memory is enough—that having just one person who loves you is a kind of magic that can't be dismissed.

And yet, she thinks, *we greedily want more.*

"Hi," Brent says, coming up beside her.

"Hey," Kara smiles.

"So what do you think?" he asks.

Kara closes her eyes and takes a deep breath. "I think... I couldn't have done this without you," she says. "And I'm extremely grateful. Thank you."

She leans in and kisses Brent on the cheek.

"You're the one people should be thanking," Brent says. "Look what you created. I'm just happy I could lend a hand."

"I saw that kiss," a familiar voice approaches Kara from the crowd. "Does Kara have a boyfriend?" her brother Jordan says as he lands right next to her.

Kara learned a long time ago she should just ignore her younger brother's taunts.

"Brent, this is my brother Jordan," Kara says. "He's a couple years younger than me. Jordan, Brent owns The Wheelhouse."

"Good to meet you," Brent says, sticking out his hand.

Jordan shakes his hand. "You too," he says. "You've got a cool place here."

"Thanks," Brent says. "It's kind of a labor of love."

"So how did you two meet?" Jordan asks.

"Wendy set us up," Kara says, smiling at Brent.

"Really?" Jordan asks. "Wendy from your work? How did she get you to agree to meeting a stranger?"

"Wendy *tricked* Kara into meeting me for coffee," Brent says.

Jordan laughs. "Now *that* makes more sense," he says. "Have you two tried Suzy's Christmas balls yet?"

"Christmas balls?" Kara asks. "That's what she's serving over there?"

"That's my name for them. She calls them 'Minnesota Fried Christmas Cookies'," Jordan says.

Kara laughs and says, "I was gonna say…"

"We'll have to give them a try," Brent says.

Kara sees Jordan become distracted by someone behind her, and she knows her brother's distraction means the conversation is over.

Kara looks where Jordan is staring, and he sees Beatrice talking with the conductor from the performance.

Figures, she thinks. *Jordan always had a thing for Beatrice.*

She turns back to Brent. "Let's go pay Suzy a visit," she says. "See you later, Jordan."

"Sounds good," Jordan says, already on his way toward Beatrice. "And nice to meet you, Brent!"

"You too," Brent says as Jordan goes out of earshot. "He seems nice," Brent says to Kara.

"My mom always says he never lets grass grow under his feet," Kara says. "He's a bit all over the place, but we love him."

Kara and Brent find their way to the canopy tent with a "Tom's Café" banner affixed to the front, and they get in line for Suzy's "Minnesota Fried Christmas Cookies".

Suzy's college friend Paul is working the register as Suzy and her boyfriend Mike fill orders in the back, occasionally delivering a skewer with three golden balls drizzled with a combination of glaze, sugar, and chocolate icing.

Laurie Banks, who works at the Kingsbury Clinic, is chatting up Paul ahead of them in line.

"Suzy is a bit of a savant with desserts," Kara says to Brent.

"Really?" Brent asks. "Do you think she'd come work for me?"

"She's going to school to be a nurse," Kara says.

"So," Brent says, "she's probably not going to come be my pastry chef?"

"Hi, Paul," Kara says as they reach the front of the line. "I see they roped you into helping."

"I volunteered," Paul says with a smile.

Suzy comes to the front of the tent to deliver an order, and Kara says, "Happy birthday, little sister."

"Thank you," Suzy says with a grin.

"Now that you've lived twenty-three years," Kara says, "what words of wisdom do you have for us?"

"Whoa," Brent says to Kara, "you're kind of putting her on the spot."

"She does this on people's birthdays," Suzy explains. "It's kind of her thing."

Kara raises her eyebrows at Brent, then looks back to Suzy. "So?" Kara asks.

"To quote Dolly Parton," Suzy says, "'Find out who you are and do it on purpose.'"

"Oh, Dolly," Kara says.

Suzy smiles, looking at the man next to her sister. "So, who's this?" she asks.

"This is Brent," Kara says. "He wants you to come work for him at The Wheelhouse."

"Oh, yeah?" Suzy asks. "How much are you paying?"

"We can negotiate," Brent says in good humor.

"Well, let me know," Suzy says, turning back to keep churning out orders of her Minnesota Fried Christmas Cookies. "I'm back in town for good!"

"No, you're not," Kara says. "What about school?"

"What about it?" Suzy says over her shoulder. "I dropped out."

"What?!" Kara asks. "You're kidding!"

"Nope," Suzy says. "I'm going to work with mom and dad at the shop, learn the ropes so I can eventually take it over."

"Okay, we're going to need to talk more about this later. But for now," Kara says, "two orders of Minnesota Fried Christmas Cookies, please!"

Twenty

Jordan and Beatrice walk side by side, scanning the crowd outside at The Wheelhouse.

"I saw her during the performance," Beatrice says. "She couldn't have gone far."

"Unless she left," Jordan says.

"She couldn't have left," Beatrice sighs. "She has to be here somewhere."

Jordan sees Jessica through a shift in the crowd. "There!" he says, pointing toward a corner on The Wheelhouse's outdoor patio.

"No, we had no idea," Jordan hears his mom say as he and Beatrice approach. "I guess he was planning this whole treasure hunt for last year's festival."

Jordan's mom and dad are sitting at a table with Jessica and his second-grade teacher, Dottie Short.

"Tom was always so talented," Dottie says. "I still have one of the poems he wrote in our second grade reading unit. I'll bring it into the Café sometime."

"Jordan!" his mom says, spotting her son. "Did you know Jessica was here?"

"Yeah," Jordan smiles, "we actually connected when she came into town earlier today."

"Did you stop and see Tom's house?" Jordan's dad says to Jessica. "Can you believe how far it's come?"

"I did," Jessica smiles. "And I'm really impressed. It's like a completely different place."

"You also need to stop by the Café before you leave town," Jordan's mom says to Jessica. "I need to treat you to a coffee—and one of Suzy's scones."

"Did you try her Christmas Cookie Kabobs?" Jordan's dad asks Jessica.

"They're called Minnesota Fried Christmas Cookies," Jordan's mom corrects her husband.

"I think 'Christmas Balls' has a better ring to it!" Dottie exclaims.

"I agree!" Jordan says.

Jessica laughs. "I did have them," she says. "All three flavors are amazing, but I especially love the gingerbread one."

Beatrice nudges Jordan, and it's time to interrupt. "Can we actually steal Jessica for a second?" Jordan asks the group.

"We need to show her something," Beatrice adds.

Jordan's mom stands up and sighs, moving toward Jessica with her arms spread for a hug. "I suppose we should go find Kara anyway," she says. "But Jessica, please don't be a stranger. You are always welcome."

"Thank you," Jessica says, turning to hug Dottie and Jordan's dad next. "And I'm taking you up on that coffee and scone," she points at Jordan's mom.

"Yes, please," Jordan's mom says in return.

When they're finally able to pry Jessica away from the group, Jordan says, "I know you said you didn't want to participate in the treasure hunt, but there's something you need to see."

Jessica sighs. "All right," she says, walking in the direction of the foot bridge. "But I have a few questions along the way."

"Done," Beatrice says.

As they walk, Jessica asks all about the performances and clue reveals throughout the week. Beatrice is a fount of knowledge, and it becomes even more obvious to Jordan that Tom may have had ideas, but they would have been nothing without Beatrice there to make them happen.

"Every single detail was absolutely perfect," Jordan says.

"Thank you," Beatrice says. "But I assure you that every single detail was *not* absolutely perfect."

"You're too close to the work," Jordan says. "I still don't understand how the angel started to float up into the sky. Or how those orchestra instruments could be outside in the cold. Or how much it must have cost to hire all those performers every night."

As they come within sight of the foot bridge, Jessica stops dead in her tracks.

"Is everything all right?" Beatrice asks.

"Yeah," Jessica says. "It's just…"

She takes a deep breath.

"Everything has changed since I was in Kingsbury last—Tom's house, the Festival," Jessica says. "This bridge still feels the same as it always has."

Jordan says, "If it's too hard—"

"It's not," Jessica says. "It's just… this is where Tom asked me out for the first time, where we had our first kiss." She pauses for a moment. "Even though I'm happy that a lot of things have changed around here, I hope this place stays the same forever, that I can always come back here."

Jordan and Beatrice stand still as Jessica closes her eyes for a moment.

When she opens them, Jessica loops one arm into Beatrice's and the other into Jordan's. Sandwiched between the two, Jessica says, "Now let's go see what Tom left in our secret spot."

Jessica navigates directly to the hidden spot in the bridge and pulls out the small box wrapped in a plastic bag. She pulls open the bag and opens the box.

Jessica smiles.

"It's an engagement ring," she says without surprise. "Tom and I talked about getting married," Jessica explains, "but he kept putting it off. He said he had to find the right way to ask me."

"Tom intended to hold the treasure hunt at last year's festival," Beatrice says. "When he was done planning it during the summer, he put a note in his will that should anything happen to him, the treasure hunt should be carried out as planned. There just wasn't enough time for me to get everything in line last year."

"I wish I would have been here to see all the performances and everything," Jessica says. "I mean, you put so much work into it!"

"What's important is that you know Tom loves you," Beatrice says.

"Oh," Jessica says with a sniffle, "I already knew that."

Jordan feels a pang in his chest.

"Now," Beatrice sighs, "I think it's extremely tacky to talk about money. But as executor of Thomas Valentine

Bell's will, I'm legally responsible to communicate that you, as the winner of the Kingsbury Christmas Festival treasure hunt, are the sole benefactor of his estate. Everything is yours."

"No," Jessica says, wiping her nose on her sleeve.

Beatrice is taken aback. "What do you mean, no?" she asks. "It's not a question."

"I mean, I'll take the cash," she says, rolling her eyes with humor, "obviously. But Tom's little fixer-upper?" She grabs Jordan by the arm. "Jordan, that house was worthless until you put some elbow grease into it. Tom bought it with a song, so it's completely paid off. Can I sign the deed over and leave everything inside to you?"

Jordan is speechless. Other than the fact he doesn't have a job to pay taxes on the property, it's a dream come true—a place to figure out his next move.

"Can you give me a *house*? Um, yes, please," he says, giving Jessica the biggest hug and even lifting her off the ground.

Jessica squeals, and after she's back on solid land, she turns to Beatrice. "Did Tom give you anything in his will?" Jessica asks.

Beatrice shakes her head. "No," she says, "just a lot of responsibility to do his bidding." She shrugs. "That's just Tom, I guess."

Jessica says, "Well, I think you should get something. Minus the house, how much in assets did Tom have?"

"He didn't have all that much for hard assets," Beatrice says. "He saved most of his money. Without the house, it's about a hundred thousand."

"Will you split it with me?" Jessica asks. And then a second later, "Actually, I'm not asking you. I'm telling you. We're splitting whatever is left in the estate after the house is signed over to Jordan. It's settled."

Beatrice just looks at Jessica.

"Use it to help pay off your student loans," Jessica says. "Tom left me a gift, and I'm regifting a portion of it to you. It's only appropriate after he made you organize a weeklong outdoor theatre production."

"It *would* be nice not to have student loans anymore," Beatrice says.

"See?" Jessica says. "Plus, I'm guessing Tom made you do other things to wrap up his unfinished business that we don't even know about."

Beatrice winces.

"I knew it," Jessica says.

"Really?" Jordan asks. "What else did he make you do?"

Twenty-One

Suzy takes stock of her pre-made cookie dough.

"We're almost out," she tells Mike. "We could maybe do a dozen more orders."

She looks at the line still queued in front of the booth, and she shoots Mike a look of concern.

"It's fine," he says. "We go until we sell out, then we enjoy the rest of the festival."

"It's a good problem to have," Paul says from the front table. "It's better to sell out than have a bunch of extra stock anyway."

Suzy shrugs, realizing the truth in this—as long as they're not losing out too big.

"Yeah," Mike says. "Besides, what do they say? Leave 'em wanting more?"

Suzy exhales. "You're both right," she concedes.

Within ten minutes they sell their final order of Minnesota Fried Christmas Cookies and close down the booth. Packing away the equipment takes a fraction of the time it took to set up, and the three slip into the crowds to enjoy whatever the Festival has left in store.

They visit the other tables with a cup of cider in hand, then roast a marshmallow or two. And what makes the whole thing sweeter for Suzy is the feeling of accomplishment.

Every so often, someone stops to rave about the Tom's Café booth this year and to share their excitement for Suzy to be back in town.

Suzy sees her mom before her mom sees her. Since she took the first half of the day off to rot in bed and then spent the second half prepping her fried Christmas cookies, Suzy successfully avoided her mom all day.

But now it's time, Suzy thinks, bracing herself.

She tells Mike and Paul she has to deal with something and approaches her mom.

"There's my birthday girl," Suzy's mom says, pulling Suzy in for a hug. "The fried treats were a smash. And a much better idea than the usual platters of Christmas cookies we usually sell."

"People seem to have liked them," Suzy says. "But maybe they're just being nice."

"Oh no," Suzy's mom says, "not in this town."

"What do you mean?" Suzy asks.

"People always say that everybody is so 'Minnesota Nice' and everything," she says. "Maybe that's true when Minnesotans are dealing with tourists and visitors, but when they're dealing with their own neighbors, they're downright cruel sometimes. Being in business for thirty years, I could tell some stories." She shakes her head. "But I suppose you'll find out for yourself when you take over the shop."

Suzy stops, confused at what she just heard. "What do you mean?" she asks.

"Your dad told me about school," Suzy's mom says. "Suze, I have to tell you that I'm disappointed."

Suzy feels a tightness rise in her chest, the kind that causes her to put her guard up. "It just wasn't right for me," she says. "I was doing it for all the wrong reasons, and I couldn't—"

"I'm not disappointed that you quit school," her mom says, "although that is a major decision not without consequences." She takes a deep breath. "I'm disappointed that I made you feel like you needed to hide it from me."

"I didn't know how you'd react," Suzy says. "I mean, I was a semester away from graduating, and I pull the plug? I know how irresponsible that is."

"Maybe it is," Suzy's mom says, "but the fact you couldn't tell me? I look back at how your dad and I raised you kids, and it breaks my heart to think we did things that made you feel you couldn't share something *that* important with us, that you felt like you were on your own. I'm disappointed in *my*self that I didn't create the kind of relationship where you feel safe and loved above everything else."

"You didn't do anything intentional to make me feel unsafe or unloved," Suzy says.

"I tried not to," her mom says. "But obviously it happened along the way."

"Then that's just life," Suzy says. "No one grows up unscathed, right?"

Suzy's mom sighs. "I wish it didn't have to be like that," she says. "But... I *am* excited we'll be working together. You're a real professional, you know."

"There's always room for improvement," Suzy says. "But it's good to know I'll be learning from the best."

Suzy's mom shakes her head. "Oh, I think this will be less of a mentor-mentee situation and more of a learn-from-each-other deal."

Suzy's mom sticks out her hand.

Suzy smiles, and they shake hands.

"Welcome aboard to Tom's Café," Suzy's mom says.

***

As Suzy makes her way back to find Mike and Paul, she passes by Doug White from *The Kingsbury Gazette*. Dressed up as Santa and sitting in a sleigh, he listens intently as a little girl tells him what she wants for Christmas.

Santa gives the girl a candy cane and her dad, who Suzy recognizes as Kara's boss, lifts her off the sleigh.

Then Suzy sees Santa staring at her.

"Ho! Ho! Ho!" Santa says. "Miss Suzy, why don't you come visit Santa?"

Suzy smiles politely, trying to continue on her way. "No," she says. "But thank you, Doug."

"I insist," Santa says. "I was asked to deliver a present to you tonight."

"I'm all good with presents this year," Suzy says, thinking of the collection of unopened gifts from yesterday still on her bedroom dresser.

Santa gets off his sleigh and makes his way to Suzy. "Ho! Ho! Ho! Has Miss Suzy lost the spirit of Christmas?" he asks.

Suzy frowns at Santa. "I'm not sure I ever had it," she says, thinking of the way the hoopla of Christmas always seemed to outshine her own birthday—how it still does.

"Well," Santa says, pulling a golden box from his coat pocket, "maybe this can restore your spirits."

Suzy takes the box and inspects the little card. A simple "Twenty-Three" is scrawled in the same lilting handwriting font as her other gifts.

"Open it!" Santa bellows.

Suzy takes the lid off the box, and she pulls out a gold cookie cutter in the shape of a bell.

"A bell for Miss Suzy Bell!" Santa says.

She grins and sees a piece of paper in the bottom of the small box. She fishes it out, unfolds it, and finds the same lilting handwriting from her past week of gifts. Except this time, it's not a font. And rejoined with its perfect imperfections, she recognizes the handwriting right away.

Suzy, the note reads. *Birthdays are meant to be celebrated—and big! I don't know anyone who is more deserving of celebration than my baby sister.*

She feels tears prickle her eyes. She clears her throat as she keeps reading.

By this point, you should have received all twenty-three of my gifts. Let each and every one of them remind you that you are loved.

Suzy closes her eyes before reading the sign-off.

Forever and always your brother, Tom.

Suzy starts to cry in earnest and puts the note and cookie cutter back into the box. And she hugs Santa.

Santa holds her, and she presses her face into his red coat. After a few moments, she draws back and wipes away her tears.

"Thank you," Suzy tells Santa.

"Ho! Ho! Ho!" Santa says. And then he leans in and whispers, "Happy birthday."

***

Suzy rejoins Mike and Paul just as Kara steps up onto a table with a megaphone.

"What is she doing?" Jordan asks, appearing by Suzy's side with Beatrice and Jessica nearby.

"Making an announcement," Brent says with a smile, as he and Kara's co-worker Wendy join the group.

"If I can have everyone's attention," Kara says into the megaphone.

She gives a moment for the crowd to settle down, then Kara says, "I just want to thank everyone for coming out to the Kingsbury Christmas Festival."

Applause smatters across the crowd.

"I especially want to extend a thank you to our vendors and our host for the night, The Wheelhouse," she says, directing her own applause in Brent's direction.

"Now our time together is coming to an end, but I need to share a story and then ask for your help with something. Does that sound all right?"

Acknowledgement ripples across the crowd.

"Thirty-five years ago, the Christmas Festival was first organized in memory of Lucy Amundson, a seven-year-old girl who died of cancer the previous year." Kara clears her throat and continues, "Last year, we lost Thomas Bell, who helped organize this Festival for five years before he died in the line of duty as a paramedic. For the past several years of the Festival, we forgot to honor Lucy's memory. And the loss of Tom is an important reminder to spend time with those we still have and to honor those we've lost."

Kara sees her parents smiling up at her from amongst the crowd.

"Lucy's parents, Frank and Georgia Amundson, still live in town," Kara says. "And Frank is recovering from a heart attack in the hospital down the street. To let them know that we're honoring Lucy's memory, please join us as we walk to the hospital and sing a song in memory of Lucy."

As Kara steps down from the table, servers from The Wheelhouse make quick work of passing out electric candles and lyric sheets to the entire crowd. And in less than ten minutes, the group is positioned in front of the hospital, ready to sing.

But then Kara realizes she doesn't know how to start the song.

She's looking around the crowd for someone with any kind of singing voice to help when a young girl that Kara has never seen before appears beside her.

"Can I start the song?" the girl asks.

Kara smiles at the girl and nods. "Yes, please," she says.

And in a strong, clear voice, the girl starts singing "Silent Night" before being joined by a hundred more voices.

Up on the third floor of the hospital, Frank and Georgia Amundson hear the singing from outside and walk to the window. Down in front of the hospital, they see the entire town gathered in song—for their Lucy.

ONE YEAR LATER

Epilogue

Kara gives Brent a kiss.

"You're going to do great," Brent tells her.

She squeezes his hand three times, then walks onto the stage to cheers and applause.

Kara lifts the microphone and says, "Welcome to the Kingsbury Christmas Festival!"

The crowd gathered in Carlson Square ramps up their excitement.

"I'm Kara, and on behalf of the Kingsbury Community Club, I want to say how grateful we are that you came out to connect with your neighbors, support our small businesses, and ring in the Christmas season with some of our favorite holiday music."

The crowd gives her another round of applause.

"I am especially excited because this is the first Kingsbury Christmas Festival that fully embraces the spirit of giving. Thanks to our generous local businesses, all proceeds of the items purchased at our vendor tables tonight will go toward the Lucy Amundson and Thomas Bell Community Fund, which directly supports arts programs and projects within the Kingsbury community."

The crowd cheers again, and Kara even hears a whistle.

"This is especially close to my heart as Tom Bell's sister," Kara says. "Before we get started, I want to invite Frank Amundson to the stage to share a few words about the history of the Kingsbury Christmas Festival and what this means to him as the father of Lucy Amundson."

Frank walks onto the stage and gives Kara a hug before accepting the microphone.

Jordan takes this transition in the program as an opportunity to slip away and rejoin Beatrice at the Kingsbury Historical Society booth.

"And I turned around, and Jordan was down on his knee!" Beatrice says, extending her left hand to show Jessica her engagement ring.

Jordan comes up behind Beatrice and hugs her.

Beatrice giggles with surprise. "Hey," she says to Jordan.

"Hey," Jordan returns with a smile.

And they kiss.

"I didn't realize you were such a romantic!" Jessica says to Jordan.

"Romance-schmomance," he says with a shrug.

"How are things with the *Gazette* project?" Jessica asks.

"Actually," Jordan says, "really well."

After the final issue of the *Gazette* was published, Doug White put the building up for sale. Jordan pitched an idea to Doug, and Jordan ended up officially "buying" the business—or basically, just the name and its archives—for one dollar.

Under Jordan's direction, the *Gazette* is now published as a limited-run monthly magazine to document the evolution of Kingsbury through essays and photos. And with a massive grant from the State Historical Society, Jordan and Beatrice worked side by side to merge the archives of the Kingsbury Historical Society and *The Kingsbury Gazette* into one climate-controlled space and to digitize the entire collection. Throughout the process, Jordan and Beatrice co-authored a book outlining the history of Kingsbury from inception to present.

"We just turned in the final copy of the book to the publisher," Beatrice says.

"So when can I read it?" Jessica asks.

"You're on our list for advanced reader copies," Beatrice winks at Jessica.

"And I just saw Tom's house listed for short-term rental," Jessica says.

"Yeah," Jordan says. "It turned out really nice, and it's actually booked through the holidays."

"I think Tom would've liked that you're using his place to welcome people into Kingsbury," Jessica says.

"We were just talking about that the other day," Beatrice says with a smile. "We think so too."

"I may just have to book it while I'm in town for some house hunting," Jessica says with a smile.

It takes a couple seconds for Jordan and Beatrice to put together the pieces.

Then Beatrice yells, "You're moving back?!"

From the Tom's Café booth, Suzy laughs as she sees Beatrice and Jessica jump up and down a few canopy tents away.

"I think Jessica just shared the news," Suzy says to Paul with a smile.

Suzy and Paul are already prepping to serve more "Christmas-in-a-Cup Donut Holes" during intermission. At their pace, it's going to be a record-setting event.

After a lot of soul searching, Suzy decided to go back for spring semester and complete her nursing degree, though she stood firm in her decision not to take the board exam. Suzy and Jessica reconnected while down in the Cities and bonded over making plans to move back home. Jessica would need more time than Suzy, but they both agreed the Christmas Festival was the perfect occasion for Jessica to break the news.

"I'm surprised Jessica ever moved away from Kingsbury to start," Paul says.

"Says the newest transplant to town," Suzy jokes.

"Hey," Paul says with a shrug, "it's a nice place."

"I agree," Suzy says. "It's just different when you're from here."

"Okay, okay," Paul says, sticking his hands in the air. "But do I get extra credit for dating a local?"

Paul wraps his arms around Suzy and picks her up off the ground. "No!" she giggles. "No extra credit given!"

After graduating and passing his nursing board exam, Paul applied to and got a job at the hospital in Kingsbury. By the time he moved to town in late summer, Suzy and Mike had already gone their separate ways. Between shift work for Paul and Suzy taking on Tom's Café *and* embarking on a collaboration to provide a custom weekly dessert menu for The Wheelhouse, they both have full schedules. But they naturally fit into each other's lives.

Paul puts Suzy down, and they melt into each other as applause rises from the crowd.

"Oh," Paul says, quickly pulling away. "I forgot to tell you. I arranged a small surprise for you."

"Yeah?" Suzy asks.

Paul turns Suzy in the direction of the stage just as the curtains part to reveal a choir of twenty boys in white robes.

Suzy can hardly contain her smile when the choir—and the entire crowd—kick off the Kingsbury Christmas Festival with "Happy Birthday".

Acknowledgements

Two years ago, I created an outline of "The Bell Siblings" for a writing exercise. I tucked the story away when I decided to take a break from writing, but my brain kept revisiting the three siblings and the brother they lost. When I was finally ready to sit down and write again, their story became the book you're holding now.

I had two separate conversations that prompted me to put pen to paper and revisit the Bell siblings. After a lunch meeting one day, Vicki asked, "Have you been writing anything lately?" And over lunch two weeks later, Kala and I talked about what we want to accomplish in life. Sometimes encouragement comes in a simple question; sometimes it comes in a philosophical conversation. Either way, a big thank you to Vicki and Kala for encouraging me to keep doing something I love.

The fictional city of Kingsbury is inspired by Proctor, Minnesota. Proctor is the place that raised and shaped me, and I'm so grateful for the people and institutions that make it "home". Hopefully my fellow Proctorites can recognize the heart of our small town between the lines of this story. And thank you to the people of Proctor for creating a place I always want to come back to.

Finally, this story is about the way family members lead separate but ever-entwining lives. Thank you to my family for being entwined in my story.

Russell Habermann is an author, poet, songwriter, and visual artist. He also wrote *The Great Golden Spike Treasure Hunt*. He resides in Proctor, Minnesota.

Made in the USA
Monee, IL
26 September 2025